Liam said, "I'll be mov[...]
know I was here."

But I'll know. And she'd feel forever guilty. "At the very least, you need to stay for a couple of hours in case the cops are watching the house."

He shook his head. "It won't take much for me to sneak into the forest and disappear."

Half of her brain screamed for her to let him go. But the other half was louder and would not be ignored. This time her decision was final.

"Stay," she whispered.

"Do you believe I'm innocent?"

"This isn't about you, Liam. It's about the truth."

The stakes couldn't be higher. If she'd misjudged him and his claim of amnesia was a sham, Ava had just invited a cold-blooded killer into her life.

FUGITIVE HARBOR

CASSIE MILES

Harlequin

INTRIGUE

To all those dedicated to repairing and maintaining the Oregon lighthouses. Shine on.

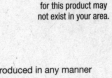

ISBN-13: 978-1-335-45719-6

Fugitive Harbor

Copyright © 2025 by Kay Bergstrom

For questions and comments about the quality of this book, please contact us at CustomerService@Harlequin.com.

TM and ® are trademarks of Harlequin Enterprises ULC.

Harlequin Enterprises ULC
22 Adelaide St. West, 41st Floor
Toronto, Ontario M5H 4E3, Canada
www.Harlequin.com

Printed in Lithuania

Cassie Miles, a *USA TODAY* bestselling author, lived in Colorado for many years and has now moved to Oregon. Her home is an hour from the rugged Pacific Ocean and an hour from the Cascade Mountains—the best of both worlds—not to mention the incredible restaurants in Portland and award-winning wineries in the Willamette Valley. She's looking forward to exploring the Pacific Northwest and finding mysterious new settings for Harlequin Intrigue romances.

Books by Cassie Miles

Harlequin Intrigue

Mountain Retreat
Colorado Wildfire
Mountain Bodyguard
Mountain Shelter
Mountain Blizzard
Frozen Memories
The Girl Who Wouldn't Stay Dead
The Girl Who Couldn't Forget
The Final Secret
Witness on the Run
Cold Case Colorado
Find Me
Gaslighted in Colorado
Escape from Ice Mountain
Shallow Grave
K-9 Hunter
Fugitive Harbor

Visit the Author Profile page at Harlequin.com.

CAST OF CHARACTERS

Ava Donovan—A trained historian/archeologist who put herself through college working on home renovations, she's hired to live on-site and restore a privately owned but abandoned lighthouse on the Oregon coast.

Dr. Liam Brody—Ava's former college professor who teaches nautical archeology specializing in shipwrecks is under house arrest, awaiting trial for murder. Desperate to solve the crime himself, he goes on the run and becomes a fugitive.

Stuart Whitcomb—Liam's partner in a salvage operation based in Newport is killed at sea from blunt force trauma. Liam, the only other person on the boat, claimed to be unconscious.

Deputy Don Jessop—The local lawman has a grudge against Ava's family and suspects she's aiding and abetting the fugitive professor.

Fish Finley—The former employee of Liam's agrees to testify at his trial that he heard Liam and Stuart arguing.

Peter Quincy—The owner of a competing salvage company and the husband of the woman who hired Ava has much to gain if Liam goes out of business.

Charles Tancredo—The harbormaster at the Bay of Newport has long been suspected of drug smuggling through British Columbia.

Chapter One

A jagged shard of lightning pierced the low-hanging clouds and streaked across the night sky above the Cape Absolute lighthouse on the Oregon coast. The bolt might have struck a tall Sitka spruce, or torn a chunk off the basalt cliffs, or spent its force plunging to the depths of the roiling Pacific. Standing at the mullioned window in the dining room of the lightkeeper's cottage, Ava Donovan touched her fingertip to the cold glass and traced the path of a raindrop down the pane. She braced for the thunder. In seconds, an explosive boom rattled her eardrums.

A lightning storm was unusual for the coast. They got plenty of rain, but only a few of the storms erupted into lightning. The celestial light show mesmerized her and sent shivers marching down her spine. Not that she was cold. Her plaid, flannel pajamas and wool socks kept her plenty warm.

She turned away from the window and padded down a short hallway to the study where a desk lamp shone on a document she'd been studying—a copy of a lightkeeper's log from the 1920s, one of the few written by a woman, Elizabeth Mayes, known as the Widow of Cape Absolute.

Ava took a seat at the rolltop desk, straightened her shoulders and shook off her tension. *Nothing to be scared of.* The lightning was odd, but rain was typical for late April when

Fugitive Harbor

the daffodils were up and rhododendrons started to bud. Night temperatures hovered in the forties. Gusting winds kicked up to thirty miles per hour. If she'd been an official lightkeeper, like Elizabeth, she would have paid attention to the tide charts and barometric readings, but she wasn't here to maintain a daily record. Her job for the next six to eight months was to renovate the buildings on this property in an accurate manner to satisfy the National Historic Landmark requirements.

Uniquely qualified, she had an MA in archeology and another in American history with a published thesis highlighting landmarks of the Pacific Northwest. In addition, she'd put herself through college working on home remodels. Happily, Ava had accepted the lighthouse project, which marked a step forward in her career, and moved into the cottage on a cliff jutting into the Pacific. The only access was an unmarked dirt road that veered off the paved route through the Siuslaw National Forest and wove through the old growth forest for 2.7 miles.

No traffic. No neighbors. No problem.

Though her family—three brothers and a sister—told her she'd be lonely, solitude didn't bother her. Still, she'd felt restless tonight, apprehensive for no particular reason. At eleven o'clock, she should have been tucked into bed. Instead, she wandered. After living here for two-and-a-half weeks, she knew her way around and left most of the lights off.

In spite of being referred to as a "cottage," the lightkeeper's residence was substantial—a two-story house that was separate from the lighthouse tower. The cottage had five bedrooms, an extra-large primary suite and three other rooms that could be converted to more bedrooms for the proposed B and B. Built in the late 1800s and refurbished several times since then, the cottage had a lot of square footage, lots of windows, lots of hallways and even a couple of secret passages, rumored to be used by ghosts of former lightkeepers.

From outside, she heard a crash.

Ava bolted to her feet and dashed back to the dining room window. Another flare of lightning illuminated the forty-eight-foot-tall tower at the edge of the headland cliff. The lighthouse stood about fifty yards away from the lightkeeper's cottage. The once proud beacon warning approaching vessels of dangerous rocks and shoals had been dark for over fifty years.

Peering into the night, she couldn't see well enough to know what caused the noise. The battery-powered light she'd installed over the lighthouse entrance wasn't very bright—just a glimmer. On a cloudy, rain-soaked night like this, moonlight provided scant illumination.

She waited for another lightning flash to give her a clearer view. An aluminum ladder had fallen outside the tower and smashed into a couple of sawhorses. Though she recalled using the ladder earlier, she couldn't imagine herself being so careless as to leave it standing unattended. A chilling thought occurred: someone else might have tampered with the ladder.

Though she didn't see a shadowy figure creeping through the night, Ava had legitimate reason for concern. Over the years, graffiti artists had literally made their mark on the whitewashed exterior of the tower. Of course, they wouldn't attempt to paint in the rain. But what about the interior? She'd purchased a lock for the door to discourage them from entering, but someone might use the cover of the storm to break inside and scrawl their mark on the walls. *Not on my watch.*

In the kitchen, she flicked on the overhead light before going out to the enclosed back porch to don a heavy-duty rain poncho over her pajamas. Rubber galoshes covered her socks. Armed with a Maglite from a shelf by the door, she turned on the back porch light and paused. Though she didn't see a vehicle parked beside her truck in the rear parking lot and hadn't heard a car approaching, intruders could have hiked through the forest.

She might be facing a vandal. An intruder. A dangerous person.

When her oldest brother—the notorious Barry Donovan—helped her move in, he warned about the dangers of a twenty-seven-year-old woman living alone in a secluded place like this. He disregarded her comment that she had practiced tai chi—which was, in fact, a martial art—for years. Moves like Cloud Hands and Grasping Bird Tail probably wouldn't stop an assailant.

Barry had taken her shopping for a gun.

Now might be the time to use it. Clumsy in galoshes, she ran through the dining room and down the hall to the desk in the study. In the lower right drawer of the old rolltop, a locked box held her brand-new Glock 48. Both Barry and the saleswoman told her it was lightweight, easy to handle and held ten rounds. To operate the weapon, she only had to aim and squeeze the trigger, unleashing the automatic safety. Just pull the trigger. *Easy enough.* Plus, the neon pink Glock gleamed with bravado.

Ava punched in the combination code to unlock the small gun safe, retrieved her weapon and checked the clip the way Barry showed her. *My phone!* She definitely needed her phone in case she had to call for backup. Taking it off the charger on the desk, she stuck the phone into the flappy pocket in her poncho and returned to the kitchen. Holding the flashlight and Glock in her left hand, she used her right to unlock the back door and pull up her hood. Glock in hand, she went down three rickety stairsteps. The wind from the northeast blew rain onto her back and shoulders, pushing her toward the lighthouse and the edge of the cliff. The crashing of waves against rock accompanied her footsteps with a primeval rhythm. The beam from her Maglite barely kept the darkness at bay.

She trudged onward. Though she'd pulled the hood over her head, rain spattered her nose and cheeks. With the hand holding the gun, she pushed her bangs off her forehead. Lightning burst across the night sky, and the trees became grasping shadows, threatening to drag her into the foreboding forest. She stumbled and fell to her knee in a puddle. Accidentally, her finger squeezed. The gun went off. An explosion rocked the air. She had fired into the dirt.

"Damn, damn, damn." She bounded to her feet and ran the last several yards, trying to ignore the twinge in her wrist from the pistol's recoil. A twenty-eight-foot aluminum extension ladder lay on its side blocking the lower portion of the closed door, but the lock remained firmly in place. Even if someone had gotten inside, they couldn't have reached out to refasten the hasp. Unless they had an accomplice. *There might be more than one of them.*

Peering through the rain at the back porch, she saw the cottage door hanging wide-open. *How could that be?* She thought she'd shut the door but had been busy juggling the gun, her phone and the flashlight. Apparently, she hadn't fastened the latch tightly enough.

Splashing through puddles, she hurried back to the cottage, climbed the three steps, entered, pulled the door closed and turned the key in the dead bolt. Off with the poncho. She hung it on a hook, kicked off her boots and returned the Maglite to its place on the shelf by the door. Still carrying her Glock, she padded into the kitchen in her damp socks. The overhead light shone on the worn green-and-yellow-patterned linoleum floor where a trail of watery footprints led into the adjoining dining room. *Trouble!* Her heart thumped heavily. While she'd been outside, an intruder must have crept into the cottage. Gaining entry might have been their plan all along.

She needed backup: 9-1-1. Her phone ought to still be in her poncho, but when she went back to the porch to look, the phone was gone. She must have dropped it when she fell or when she was running. Going outside and searching in the dark seemed futile. But calling for help seemed like the best option, even though emergency responders would take at least a half hour to get here. In the study, there was a landline and her car keys. All she needed to do was go through the kitchen to the dining room. From there, the study was down a short hallway. Place the call. Take the keys. And make a mad dash for her truck.

Cautiously, she inched toward the doorway leading to the dining room, which was dark except for faint moonlight through the windows. She reached around the corner and groped for the switch. A rustling noise crackled in her ears. She heard a shuffle, sensed his presence before he grasped her wrist and yanked hard.

Off-balance, she stumbled into the dining room. He clamped an arm around her belly and pulled her back against his chest. He easily overpowered her. Releasing her wrist, he twisted her arm and took the gun from her hand.

She inhaled and prepared to scream. Not that anyone could hear her. There were no neighbors. Just forest.

"I'm sorry, Ava."

"Who? What?"

"Let me explain."

She craned her neck and tried to see his face, but she couldn't turn her head far enough. "Who are you? How do you know me?"

"It's been a long time. Six years."

"Let me go." Her muscles tensed, but she couldn't move. He held her too tightly. His wet clothing soaked her flannel pajamas."Just relax."

"Tell me who you are?"

"You came after me with a gun. Let's make sure we're on the same page. Okay?" His tone softened, but his grasp stayed firm. "Six years ago, how old were you?"

"Twenty-one."

"Where were you?"

"Eugene." She'd been in grad school at the University of Oregon, working on her MA in archeology. She couldn't imagine why he was asking these mundane questions but figured the conversation might work in her favor. If she kept him talking, he might relax his grip, and she could escape. She asked, "Were you at U of O? Are you a Duck? Did we have a class together?"

"You wore your long, dark hair in a ponytail. You've cut it."

He knew her name, knew what she looked like. "Have you been stalking me?"

"Hell, no." He sounded offended as though he wasn't the sort of man who stooped to stalking. "I saw an article in the *Register* when you signed on for this project. And a recent photo."

She glanced toward the hallway that led to the study. If she could get there, she'd lock the door and make her call. There had to be something in that rolltop she could use as a weapon.

"I remember," he said, "you were an excellent swimmer. And diver."

His mention of her water skills was a clue. "We both must have been in the nautical archeology course that studied shipwrecks near Coos Bay."

"You were the only woman in the class."

"Yeah, I was popular."

A chuckle rumbled in his chest, and she felt his grip loosen. *This is my chance.* She jabbed her left elbow into his gut and dodged to the right, slipping out of his clutches and falling to the floor. Though she wanted to go left, she was facing the opposite direction. On hands and knees, she crawled frantically toward the light in the kitchen.

He followed. Before she got very far, he grabbed her arms and pulled her up. Though caught, Ava didn't quit. She kept wriggling, fighting to free her arms and wildly kicking back at him. *To no avail.* He lifted her as though she weighed no more than a rag doll and carried her to a straight-back chair at the kitchen table. After he sat her in the chair, he stepped back a pace.

In the overhead light, she stared up at him. Her jaw dropped. "Professor Brody?"

"Are you okay? I didn't mean to hurt you."

"Why did you hide? You grabbed me. Why?"

"The gun." He reached behind his back and took her pink Glock from where he'd stashed it in the waistband of his jeans. Her lethal weapon looked tiny in his large hand. "When I heard gunfire, I didn't want to take the chance that you'd shoot first and ask questions later."

His response almost made sense. *Almost.* "Is there some logical reason why you couldn't come to the door—like a normal person—and ring the buzzer?"

"Would you have let me in?"

She pinched her lips in a tight, angry line and looked away from him, unwilling to be influenced by the glow emanating from his stormy gray eyes—eyes she remembered much too well. She'd spoken to him on the phone less than two weeks ago and couldn't believe she hadn't instantly recognized his voice. "I'd have slammed the door in your face."

"Haven't changed your mind."

"No."

Dr. Liam Brody placed her gun on the stained, cracked, beige tile countertop. "I need your help, Ava. But I'll understand if you refuse. You don't owe me anything."

As she stared at him, her firm resolve weakened. He had a mesmerizing effect on people, particularly on her. "If you understand that I don't want to get involved, why are you here?"

"I hope you'll give me a chance. Will you, at least, listen to me?"

Six years ago, she'd imagined herself in love with this tall, darkly handsome professor. They'd flirted and teased but kept a distance, except for one night when they were out on the dive boat, drinking beer on the deck and watching starlight dance across the waves. He embraced her. The warmth from his body raised her temperature several degrees, and she melted like chocolate in a double boiler. His kiss took her breath away.

Too quickly, he had turned away and apologized. An intimate relationship between professor and student was inappropriate. He never touched her again, much to her disappointment.

For years, his likeness had haunted her dreams. Liam Brody was educated, accomplished and looked great in his black wet suit with orange markings. Back then he was only thirty—young for a PhD—and had garnered international renown for the archeological reclamation of shipwrecks in the Strait of Juan de Fuca between Washington state and Canada. On the U of O campus, he'd been kind of a celebrity. A documentary crew had covered his accomplishments and praised him to the skies.

Recent news reports about him weren't so complimentary.

He was charged with murder.

"Is it true, Liam? Did you kill Stuart Whitcomb?"

"I don't think so. But I don't know for sure."

She'd followed the reports on his arrest and had heard that his defense centered on not remembering what happened. Certainly, that was a possible explanation. Amnesia often occurred in cases of trauma, especially when accompanied by a bout of unconsciousness. Still, selective forgetting seemed like an awfully convenient alibi for an accused murderer. "My sister is good friends with Stuart's ex-wife."

"I know. Stuart grew up in your hometown."

That coincidence was, of course, the reason he'd come to her for help. As a lifelong resident of Narcissus, she knew the ins and outs, the disasters and the triumphs of that small town on the Yaquina River. The Donovan family was an intrinsic part of the community. Her oldest brother had frequent confrontations with the local police, usually while drunk. Jerome, her youngest brother was a contractor who she'd hired to work on the lighthouse. Unlike Barry, he had a reputation as a hardworking, well-behaved pillar of the community with a wife and kids. Memories of the brother between those two, Michael, filled her mind and clenched her heart. Michael was eight years older than Ava who was the youngest. Shortly after he turned eighteen, he had been accused of murdering his girlfriend and wrongly convicted, sentenced to life in prison.

Ava had only been ten years old, too young to help her brother. All she could do was cry herself to sleep every night. It took twelve years to discover fresh DNA evidence proving his innocence. When he finally came home, she made it her mission to support him in spite of the townspeople and former friends who sneered at an ex-con even though he'd been proven innocent. When Michael decided to leave Narcissus and start over someplace new, she begged him to stay, offered to come with him and help out. She'd been twenty-four, old enough to make a difference in his life.

He refused to take her along. She'd just completed her university studies and had several relevant jobs and research studies lined up. Her life was going well, and Michael didn't want to disrupt her progress. He was proud of her. Told her how much her acceptance meant to him while he was incarcerated.

She'd always known he wasn't a murderer. Never ever stopped believing in him.

And now, there was Dr. Brody—a man in a similar predicament. If he wasn't guilty, she needed to take the risk and try to help him. If someone had stepped up and supported her brother, his life would have been different.

"I'll listen," she said, "but you'd better talk fast."

Chapter Two

With his thumbs hitched in the pockets of his wet jeans, Liam Brody leaned against the kitchen cabinets and studied Ava, remembering the way she'd looked six years ago with her long, curly, chestnut brown ponytail and striking blue eyes. He liked the new chin-length haircut with bangs that framed her triangular face and dimpled chin. Even though her mad dash through the storm left her disheveled, she kept her poise.

He needed to convince this cool, levelheaded woman to take his side. Grabbing her in the dark hadn't been a real smooth way to reintroduce himself, and he was lucky that she hadn't snatched her pink Glock off the kitchen counter-top and shot him in the ass.

She went out the back door to the porch and came back wearing a faded red hoodie over her pajamas. "It feels like I'm missing something important. Aren't you in the middle of a trial?"

"Correct."

"Are you out on bail?"

"Correct, again."

"Do your terms of bail allow you to come out here to the coast? Shouldn't you be wearing one of those ankle brace-lets to monitor your location?"

"I'm not allowed to go more than ten miles away from

Eugene. And I should be wearing a GPS tracking anklet. I took it off. Before you ask, that's illegal." He might as well give her all the bad news at once. "There are probably police, deputies and US marshals looking for me right now. I abandoned my car twelve miles up the coast and cut through the forest."

"You're a fugitive," she clarified.

"If it turns out that I killed Stuart, I'll do my time. But if not…"

"Wait a minute!" Her blue eyes narrowed to slits. "By allowing you to stay here at the lighthouse, I'm harboring a fugitive. Also illegal?"

"Correct."

"And you can't even tell me that you didn't kill the guy."

"Here's what I remember."

"This had better be good," she said, "or our conversation is over right now."

He'd recited this account dozens of times for the police and attorneys. The words rolled out like a well-worn mantra. "Stuart and I were out on a thirty-nine-foot-long cabin cruiser with all the bells and whistles. A classy little rig."

"Alone?" she asked.

"Yes."

"Were other boats nearby?"

"We'd gone five or six miles from the marina. I didn't notice anybody else. We were considering buying this midsize craft for our fleet. We shared ownership of the salvage company: BW Deep Dive. I'm majority shareholder with 51 percent."

"I knew you worked together on some projects. Didn't know you were partners." She nodded. "So you were on the boat. Then what happened?"

"I felt woozy, sat down. My head was spinning, then I

blacked out. Maybe I was drugged. Earlier, I drank a beer from a bottle and had a sandwich."

She held up her hand to stop his narrative. "Did the police test the food for drugs?"

"Yeah, and they didn't find anything." To his mind, the lack of drugs didn't mean much. The killer could have tossed the beer bottle overboard.

"What about you? Did they run a tox screen to see if there were drugs in your system?"

"By the time they got around to taking those tests, it was several hours later. Too long to come up with definitive results."

Her gaze leveled as she studied him. "Tell me the truth, Liam. Are you on any sort of medication? Do you take recreational drugs?"

"Not since I was eighteen." He'd lost both his mom and his best friend to drug overdoses. Not at the same time but close enough to make him a lifetime member of twelve-step programs for people who have had their lives overturned by drugs or alcohol. "Anyway, when I woke up, the motors were off, and we were drifting. Stuart had collapsed near the helm and was bleeding from a head wound."

"From what I recall reading about the case, he wasn't shot. Correct?"

"The autopsy said his injury was the result of blunt force trauma, but I didn't see a club or anything else that could have been used to whack him."

"Wouldn't be difficult to dispose of the murder weapon," she said.

He continued, "I tried CPR and called the Coast Guard. Too late. Stuart was dead by the time they arrived."

"From what I've read on the internet, you two guys weren't

all that friendly. Witnesses reported that you fought about the direction of your work together."

"We're explorers," he said, unable to keep a note of pride from his voice. Liam appreciated his ability to make a living from the sea. "I was interested in research. Stuart wanted to do more salvage. And, yeah, we argued."

She stepped past the mid-century modern kitchen table that would have been worth something if it had been in better condition and walked to the avocado-colored stove that matched the fridge—a vintage 1950s look but not historical. This place would require careful refurbishing to be designated a national landmark.

Her movements were deliberate as she filled a teapot with tap water, flicked on the front burner and moved the pot onto the flame. "It's your contention that you were drugged, but you don't know how or who did it. And then, while you were unconscious, another person boarded the cruiser and killed Stuart. Again, you don't know who or how."

"That's an accurate summary." Six years ago, she'd been in his class, and he'd been aware of her talent for logical thinking. Also, he'd been impressed by her smile, her athletic body and those beautiful blue eyes. She was the only student who tempted him to break the rules. He cleared his throat. "That's the starting point for our investigation. Are you game?"

"So far. But I want to know more."

"I'm glad we'll be working together." A few years after she graduated, he'd tried to contact her and discovered she was living with a guy. "Is that going to be a problem? I heard you had an arrangement with a lawyer in Portland."

"Portland Jimmy the urban jerk." She gave a dismissive snort. "We've been off and on for a long time, and we broke up for good a couple of months ago. He wanted a woman who liked to throw dinner parties and keep his condo clean. I preferred excavating at the Chinookan village or studying basketry from the Klamath Tribes or upgrading markers on the Lewis and Clark Trail."

Liam knew from experience that no mere human male could compete with the passion for archeological field study. "Then you got this project."

"I campaigned for the job, spent a lot of time with Georgina Solomon, the great-granddaughter of George Solomon, the lumber baron who bought the lighthouse in 1956. I think one of the main reasons she hired me was my connection to Narcissus. Georgina liked using a local. I think her husband, Peter Quincy, also runs a salvage business from Newport."

"I'm aware." Liam considered Quincy, a competitor, to be one of his primary suspects. "He and Stuart worked some deals together. I think Quincy was smuggling."

The teakettle screeched on the stove. She lifted it off the flame. Given the fact that he'd just admitted to being a fugitive, described a suspicious scenario for Stuart's murder and cast aspersions on the husband of her employer, her composure was admirable. In a calm voice, she asked if he'd prefer herbal tea or coffee. Sugar? Milk? While she prepared their beverages—chamomile tea for her and coffee through a French press for him—she said nothing. She placed their mugs on the kitchen table, produced a package of chocolate chip cookies and sat in the straight-back chair across from him.

"Here's the deal, Liam. You could be taken back into custody at any moment."

"True." And his cushy time under house arrest would be over. If the US Marshals caught up with him, Liam would likely be incarcerated, having proven himself a flight risk.

He kept those fears to himself and sipped his coffee. Caffeinated heaven.

"Level with me," she said. "Tell me about the investigating you've done so far."

"I started by hiring a PI, Wyatt Willis. He wasn't much help but still better at gathering evidence than the police. They came up empty-handed." Since he'd been confined to his house, he couldn't track down witnesses and set up interviews. "And I went to a psychologist who specializes in hypnotism to test me and find out if my subconscious mind picked up any clues."

"Psychic investigating. Awesome." She tasted her chamomile and licked her lips. "I'm guessing the hypnotist didn't figure anything out."

"Bits and pieces that don't make sense. What I need is more research, more investigation. And you're good at that."

"I appreciate the compliment, but I'm not Sherlock Holmes." She shook her head. "Let's get real. I'm not even Nancy Drew."

"But you know people in Narcissus, Stuart's hometown. His mom is still there, but his dad took off with a trophy wife and lives in Hawaii. Stuart has a sister, also in Narcissus." He knew Ava would be an asset. "Because you're a local, these people will talk to you."

"Not necessarily. His mother and sister consider themselves to be more elite than the Donovan family. For the most part, the Whitcombs aren't nice folks. Wouldn't surprise me if mom or sis popped old Stuart." When a sly grin spread across her face, he remembered why he'd found her so attractive. "His sister dated my oldest brother, Barry. Didn't end well. He wrecked her BMW."

"Is Barry the brother you used to work for?"

"No, that's Jerome. He's settled down with a wife and two

kids. He still does contract construction work, specializing in renovations. Matter of fact, he and his crew are working here. Also, I have a sister, Rachel, with two more kids. And another brother who is single."

A shadow darkened her expression. He suspected something in her family history had hurt her deeply. "What is it, Ava? What's wrong?"

"Don't want to talk about it." She took another sip of tea. "Rachel and her family still live in Narcissus."

"You mentioned her before. She's friends with Stuart's ex-wife."

"Do you know the ex?"

"I've met Holly. Been to a couple of parties where she was a guest." She hadn't made much of an impression on him until recently when she showed her blatant greed. "She expects to inherit Stuart's shares in Deep Dive. Actually, the estate and business go to his son, and she'll be the executrix which gives her a lot of control of the funds. He never got around to changing his will after their divorce."

"Sounds like a good motive for bumping him off."

"She has an airtight alibi. At the time of Stuart's murder, Holly was on an Alaskan cruise."

"Hush." Ava went silent. For a tense moment, she listened, then she pushed away from the table and ran across the linoleum to the windows in the dining room. "I see headlights in the front parking area."

"How could you hear cars approaching over the rain and wind?"

"I'm accustomed to the silence. I don't get many visitors." Her voice quavered. "Two vehicles. A cop car and an official-looking van."

He couldn't believe the police were able to track him so fast. He'd ditched his phone and ankle bracelet. While he was

driving from Eugene, he'd taken a circuitous route and abandoned his car before hiking twelve miles through the forest.

"How did they know?" He shook his head. "I didn't tell
anybody I was coming here."

"Two weeks ago, you called me," she said. "No doubt your
phone was monitored."

"I used a burner."

"For somebody who isn't a criminal, you're kind of clever."

"Thank you," he said.

"Not a compliment." She stepped up to confront him.
"You convinced me. I want to know more about your investigation. What can I do to help?"

"Don't turn me over to the police."

Chapter Three

Moments after she'd seen the headlights, Ava scurried through the first floor of the lightkeeper's cottage to the entryway. The doorbell buzzed insistently and a heavy fist pounded on the solid oak door, which was one of the few architectural features she didn't need to replace. Details on the intricate carving of a double-masted schooner at full sail were still clearly defined. Clutching her red sweatshirt closed to hide her pajamas, she opened the door. The porchlight illuminated two men, sheltering from the rain under the triangular portico.

She recognized Deputy Don Jessop, a Lincoln County officer, from the many times he'd visited her family's home while she was growing up, usually to harass or arrest Barry. Standing in the storm with his buck teeth bared and rain dripping from the tip of his long nose, he looked as angry as a carnivorous weasel. From Barry's first run-in with the law in ninth grade, Jessop had picked on her linebacker brother who had a big mouth to match his broad chest and bad attitude.

The other man was tall and lean with a thick gray mustache that reminded her of her dad, a quiet, decent man who did his best to support his large family but died before she really got to know him. The guy on the porch wore a five-pointed badge on his dark gray rain jacket. The brim of his black cowboy hat shaded his deep-set eyes. "Are you Ava Donovan?"

"I am. And you are?"

"Deputy US Marshal Todd Woodburn."

Though Barry taught her to stand up to law enforcement and never show fear, Ava knew better than to be rude. She wanted this encounter to be over quickly, preferably before they sniffed out the entrance to the secret passage where Liam was hiding. Infusing her tone with righteous indignation to mask her nervousness, she asked, "Why are you here?"

"This conversation would be easier if we were inside," the marshal said.

Should she ask for a search warrant or would that make her look guilty? She blurted, "What do you want?"

"There's an escaped fugitive in the area, and we need to make sure you're safe."

Concern for her safety sounded rational. She couldn't think of a reason to refuse.

After they'd tromped inside and wiped their boots on the mat by the door, she indicated a series of hooks where they could hang their coats. Both men declined her offer, which she considered good news, an indication that they didn't intend to stay long. She might get out of this situation without being arrested. Her fingers wrapped around the neon pink Glock tucked into her sweatshirt pocket.

Jessop looked down his pointy nose and sneered. "I should have known that a Donovan would be involved in this."

"Involved in what?" She glared at the deputy. "Has something happened to my family? Is something wrong?"

"There's so much wrong with you people that I can't list it all." He turned toward Marshal Woodburn and continued, "Her oldest brother has been arrested a dozen times. Another brother spent twelve years in prison for murder."

A burst of anger eclipsed her anxiety. "Michael was released. Wrongly accused and convicted due to incompetence from the officers in your jurisdiction. You made mistakes, and my brother paid the price. He's received some compensation from the state of Oregon, and the Exoneration Network, that's ExNet, is working to get more. A lot more."

"A waste of taxpayers' money."

Her fingers twitched near the trigger of the Glock. Might be worth jail time to shoot this guy. Barry had always referred to Deputy Don Jessop as Jess-hole, and she had to pinch her lips together to keep from shouting the insult. Stiffly, she said, "Get out of my house."

"Not your house. Don't belong to you."

"Get out."

"First, I got a couple of questions," Jess-hole said. "We saw your lights when we parked. You're out of bed in the middle of the night. How come?"

"I wasn't aware that being awake was against the law."

Woodburn took off his cowboy hat and smoothed his thinning gray hair off his forehead. "We got off on the wrong foot, Ms. Donovan. Let's start over. I don't want to leave you here alone when you might be in danger."

"I won't tolerate insults to my family."

"I'm sure Deputy Jessop is sorry." Woodburn held up his hand, blocking any comment from Jess-hole. Though the federal marshal didn't have command in Lincoln County, he was clearly in control. "This is an unusual house."

"The lightkeeper's cottage," she said.

"But the lighthouse has been decommissioned."

"Hasn't been lit since 1976. The owner, Georgina Solomon Quincy intends to apply for status as a National Historic Landmark."

"Yeah, yeah, yeah." Jess-hole cleared his throat. "Still

doesn't explain why you're up and pacing around. Maybe you're hiding somebody in here."

"Not that I owe you an explanation," she said, "but I was in the study doing research, reading the lightkeeper's log of Elizabeth Mayes, the Widow of Cape Absolute, written in the 1920s. Her husband was lost at sea, and she took over his job. According to legend, she stood on the platform of the widow's walk at the upper level of the lighthouse and kept watch every night. The double-masted schooner carved on the front door is meant to represent the missing vessel."

Woodburn nodded. "I can tell that you love your work."

"I do," she said. "The history of a place informs and explains the present."

Unlike Jess-hole, the federal marshal seemed intelligent. His dark eyes scanned the entryway and the staircase leading to the second-floor bedrooms. He peered into the large living room with the old, worn furniture, threadbare rugs and carved rocking chairs set in front of a rugged, stone fireplace. After taking his time to carefully examine his surroundings, he turned his attention back to her. "Your socks are damp. Have you been out in the rain?"

Though Ava wasn't good at lying, Barry had coached her. He'd told her the most effective deception was based on telling as much of the truth as possible. *Honesty is the best policy, right?* Besides, she couldn't very well deny that she'd gone outside to look around when water splotched all over the floor. "I heard a crash near the lighthouse and went to investigate."

"What caused the noise?"

"Earlier today, I was doing work with a ladder and left it leaning against the tower. The wind must have blown it down, but I couldn't see from here." She'd spoken the truth but felt like she had a flashing red light on her forehead proclaiming her a liar. "I'm nervous about intruders."

"Why?"

"Graffiti," she said. "Vandals scrawled all over the outside of the lighthouse, but the interior is unmarked. I worried that they might use the cover of the storm to break in."

The federal marshal held her in a suspicious state of scrutiny. "If you had encountered an intruder, how did you intend to protect yourself?"

Outsmarted. He'd set a trap for her, and she'd jumped in with both feet. Holding her Glock 48 with two fingers, she lifted the weapon from her sweatshirt pocket. "I'm armed."

Jessop whipped his gun from the holster and aimed it, two-handed, at her. "Gun on the floor. Hands on your head. Do it. Now."

Staring down the bore of his over-size sidearm, she didn't think of the deputy as a joke. As dangerous as the furry but deadly wolverines that had begun to establish colonies in Deschutes County, Jessop scared her. She looked from him to the marshal. Slowly, she held the gun toward Woodburn. "Take it."

Woodburn gently removed the Glock from her two-finger hold and lifted it to his nose. "This weapon has been recently fired."

While she bobbed her head, Jessop holstered his gun and roughly spun her around. He yanked her right wrist behind her back and twisted until she yelped. Then he snapped on a handcuff. "You have the right to remain silent."

"That's enough," Woodburn said. "Release her."

"She pulled a gun on us," Jessop whined. "She can't do that."

From the corner of her eye, she saw Woodburn dangling

her pink weapon. "Did this nasty, little Barbie Glock scare you?"

"You said she fired it."

"It was an accident," she said.

He kept hold of her arm and shook her. "Explain yourself, Ava Donovan."

"Let go of me."

"Not until you promise to be a good girl." He sounded like he was enjoying himself. Causing her pain gave him pleasure, and there wasn't anything she could do to stop him.

Without raising his voice, Woodburn gave the orders. "Deputy, remove the handcuff. Then I want you to go upstairs and search. Look in every closet and under every bed."

Jessop hadn't been terribly rough, but she still felt violated. She rubbed her wrist where the handcuff had been. "I never gave you permission to search."

"I told you so," the deputy said. "She's hiding something."

"I just don't want you pawing through my things with your grubby hands," Ava said. "Marshal, please do the right thing."

"You're within your rights to demand a warrant," Woodburn said. "It'll take a couple of hours for us to locate a judge in the middle of the night. Could be damn inconvenient. We could be here all night."

She hated that idea. "Maybe you can go upstairs with the deputy and supervise."

Jessop glared at her. "I promise not to touch your precious things. I'm on the hunt, looking for a fugitive."

The thought of him in proximity to her clothes, perfume and mementos sickened her, but she supposed it would be worth it to get rid of these two. "Don't touch anything."

While he clomped up the stairs, she turned to Woodburn.

"I suppose you want to look around down here. I can give you a tour."

"I appreciate your courtesy." He fell into step beside her as she led the way through the lower level. A large living room stood opposite the dining room. Down the hallway was a sitting room, a nursery and a game room—one or more of which would be converted into bedrooms for the B and B. In the kitchen, there was a breakfast nook and a huge pantry, well stocked to provide meals for the crew working on the renovations.

She looked up toward the ceiling. "Shouldn't Deputy Jessop be done by now?"

"Soon enough," Woodburn said. "You told us that history shapes and predicts present events."

Not exactly what she'd said, but close. "Go on."

"I'm curious, Ms. Donovan. What does past experience tell you about the murder of Stuart Whitcomb?"

"I don't have enough information," she said, quickly and honestly. "I know he grew up in my hometown of Narcissus and wasn't well-liked. Other than that, I've followed media reports on the trial. Just like everybody else."

"The accused murderer is someone you know," Woodburn said. "A former professor of yours. Liam Brody. Do you recognize the name?"

"Of course. Professor Brody was an excellent teacher and a decent human being. When I heard he was arrested, I couldn't believe it."

"His car was abandoned near here."

Liam had told her it was hidden behind a storefront. How did they locate it so quickly? "Did somebody follow him?"

"The vehicle has a GPS tracker."

That explained it. "I haven't seen a car."

"According to my information, you talked to him on the phone a few weeks ago."

Apparently Liam's strategy of using a burner had been unsuccessful. Law enforcement probably had his house bugged. "He called," she admitted. "And he wanted to chat about people in my hometown. I wished him luck on the trial but didn't know anything that would be useful in his defense. Stuart's family and mine ran in different circles."

"Ms. Donovan, I'll need to see the paperwork for your gun."

While she led him down the hallway, her heart pumped faster with every step. In the study, the secret passageway was accessed by unfastening hidden hinges on a floor-to-ceiling bookcase that turned outward to allow access. Inside the closet-sized space with a ladder leading to the second floor, Liam was hiding. If he sneezed or dropped his coffee mug, Marshal Woodburn would tear out the books and claw through the fake wall.

Purposely, she looked away from the entrance to the passageway and concentrated on the rolltop desk. "Here's the lightkeeper's daily log written by Elizabeth Mayes. This is actually a copy. The original pages are too fragile to leave the research library at the Oregon Historical Society Museum."

He perused the handwritten notations that included time, temperature, barometric pressure, wind velocity and so forth. In addition, Elizabeth added personal notes, ranging from a sighting of a family of river otters in the Yaquina to a lover's dream of her missing husband. Ava had considered starting a daily log of her own. Lots of people followed that procedure to keep track of events. She'd have to ask Liam if he had a captain's log.

"Where do you keep your gun?" the marshal asked. "And why pink?"

As she opened the locked lower drawer and showed him her gun safe that also held her registration and paperwork, she explained, "I don't know anything about weapons, but my brother talked me into getting one so I'd be safe. The neon pink made me feel less frightened. I haven't been to a firing range yet, but I'd better get some practice."

"You don't want any other accidents." He ejected the clip from the weapon. "Here are a couple of tips. Don't keep your gun loaded. Also, you need to store the ammunition separately."

"Yes, sir." The marshal seemed so calm and natural. She wanted to believe that he'd help her and Liam. "Earlier you agreed with me when I said the past provides a foundation for the present and the future."

"I believe that."

"Do you think the motive for Stuart's murder could be something that occurred a long time ago and has nothing to do with Professor Brody?"

"Do you?"

"I don't know." If she'd learned anything from Michael's wrongful conviction, it was that the initial investigation needed to be completely, utterly, totally comprehensive. The truth might hinge on a seemingly inconsequential detail. "The police need to do more digging into Stuart's background. And his family's history."

"My job doesn't include investigation," Woodburn said. "In this case, the US Marshal Service was contacted by the Oregon State Police for assistance in guarding and transporting Liam Brody while he's on trial."

She'd never really understood the layers of legal and judicial bureaucracy, but since Woodburn was an officer, it seemed like he ought to be a crime-solver. "What if you uncovered evidence that proved his innocence?"

"My task is to locate and arrest the fugitive." He placed her gun in the small safe, closed the drawer and locked it.

"But what if—"

"I'm good at my job, Ms. Donovan. Like they say in the Mounties, I always get my man."

Not this time, Marshal.

Chapter Four

Thus far, the unwarranted search in the lightkeeper's cottage had taken thirty-three minutes according to Liam's glow-in-the-dark dive watch. He'd spent the whole time tucked inside the secret passage behind the floor-to-ceiling bookcase in the study, breathing the thick, damp air until his lungs felt clogged. The enclosed space reminded him of an elevator shaft, six feet deep and five feet wide. The height stretched two stories high, all the way from the ground floor to the attic above the upstairs level. Using his pocket Maglite, he studied the unfinished wood and two-by-four wall studs.

He closed his eyes and tried to imagine how the secret passage fit into the overall floorplan for the cottage. On one side, there was a linen closet that opened into the hallway. A small bathroom next to the kitchen bordered the other side.

With his ear pressed against the thick wall of books, he concentrated hard, straining to hear what was being said in the study and entryway. From what he could tell, Deputy Jessop—a Lincoln County officer he'd never met—held a grudge against the Donovan family, especially Ava's ne'er-do-well brother. Jessop's rude attitude toward Ava irritated Liam.

On the other hand, Woodburn showed himself to be a fairly decent guy. No surprise. Liam had already drawn that conclusion. The marshal had been escorting Liam back and forth to hearings, depositions and court dates since his arraignment. These trips started with Liam being shackled and cuffed behind the wire-mesh barrier between the front seat and the prisoner transport section in Woodburn's official US Marshals van. Now Liam was allowed to ride in the passenger seat with only a pair of standard-issue handcuffs. Though definitely not friends, they'd developed a cordial relationship. When the marshal told Ava that he wasn't an investigator, Liam understood. Woodburn didn't care about guilt or innocence. His duties revolved around transport, and he made sure Liam arrived at all required appointments in a timely manner.

The marshal's single-minded focus made him a far greater threat than Jessop, who didn't seem capable of locating his toes at the ends of his feet. When Jessop was sent to search in the upstairs, Liam worried. The second-floor exit from the secret passage emerged inside Ava's bedroom closet. The hinges for the escape hatch were more noticeable than those for the bookcase in the study. Liam climbed a crude ladder—two-by-fours nailed to wall studs—to the second-floor ledge and peeked through a narrow crack between the boards while Jessop bumbled through Ava's bedroom, muttering to himself. Liam held his breath while the deputy yanked the closet door wide and poked his head inside. He flipped through the clothes on hangers and smirked at the row of shoes lined up on the closet floor, purposely mixing two matching shoes. Then he clomped out the closet door, leaving it open.

For the time being, Liam was safe. He climbed down to the main floor.

When the two officers and Ava went to the kitchen for a cup of tea, he couldn't hear their conversation and had a mo-

ment to consider where he'd spend the night. The secret passage would work, but the tiny space was uncomfortable. He
could barely stretch out on the floor. After Jessop and Woodburn left, he might risk sleeping in one of the many bedrooms. Not really a good option. Ava hadn't welcomed him
with open arms and just might tell him to get lost. In a bedroom, he'd be vulnerable if they returned. And he couldn't
help leaving traces of himself in fingerprints and fibers that
might implicate Ava.

That left the lighthouse.

Earlier tonight in the midst of the storm, he'd tried to access the interior of the tower. He climbed the aluminum ladder to reach one of the narrow windows halfway up, about
twenty feet off the ground. The glass had been broken from
the window frame, and he peered inside using his flashlight.
Darkness obscured most of the architectural details, but he
saw damage to the winding staircase that hugged the outer
wall. Several stairsteps were broken or missing, especially
near the bottom. Just below the window, a four-foot section
had been torn from the wall, making it impossible to climb
to the highest point where the beacon had been housed when
the lighthouse was functional. If he could reach that upper
level, which was surrounded by a metal widow's walk outside the windows, it would be a decent hideout.

Fearing he might be caught, he'd taken off his backpack
and reached through the window to stash it on the busted
stairs where it couldn't be seen from the floor below. If Ava
told him to hit the road, he could retrieve his pack without
too much trouble. And if she allowed him to stay—*please,
please let that happen*—he'd come back to the lighthouse
to access his laptop, his notes on the investigation and other
personal items.

Huddled against the wall in the passage, he heard a door

slam. A moment later, Ava spoke quietly outside the bookshelf. "Liam, are you okay?"

"A little cramped. Are they gone?"

"No, they just went out to look at the lighthouse. I told them there was nothing to see and gave them the key to unlock the door. They'll be back in a few minutes."

A knife-edge of fear sliced through his already shredded composure. If Woodburn somehow managed to locate Liam's backpack, they were in big trouble. "Are they suspicious?"

"Oh, yeah. Woodburn noticed the grounds in the French press I used to make your coffee."

A good thing he'd taken his mug into the passageway. "What did you tell him?"

"Told him that I'd prepared coffee for myself, then changed my mind about drinking the caffeine and dumped it in the sink. I'm not sure he believed me."

He heard her suck down an anxious breath and regretted putting her in this difficult situation. "Anything else?"

"They tracked your car with a GPS bug and listened to our conversation on the burner phone. Marshal Woodburn is smart, really smart."

He noticed a note of confusion in her tone. "And?"

"On some level, it feels like he's on your side. He made a comment about understanding how the past might lead to a solution in the present. As if researching Stuart's background could result in useful evidence."

"I overheard a piece of that conversation when you were here in the study." During the time he'd spent in Woodburn's van, Liam had gotten the impression that the marshal wasn't impressed with the evidence, or lack thereof, compiled by the local police.

"He also asked if you or Stuart were friends with Peter Quincy or Charles Tancredo."

"I wouldn't say we were friends, but we know each other." Quincy was Georgina's husband and Tancredo was the harbormaster at the Port of Newport. He managed both the commercial docks and the recreational marina. "Why?"

"Something about trafficking illegal cargo."

"Drugs." Cartels operating from Mexico to the south distracted from the northern border with Canada where gangs and organized criminals took advantage of less stringent surveillance. "Stuart wasn't a law-abiding person, but he wasn't a fool. I can't imagine how or why he'd get involved with drug dealers."

"Still, his murder sounds kinda like a hit. Don't you think?" Before he could comment about her unexpected familiarity with cartel violence, she gave a squeak and said, "Gotta go. Woodburn and Jess-hole are back."

Jess-hole? He liked the nickname.

From the kitchen, he heard murmurs of their conversation. As he listened, the three of them made their way through the hallways to the front door. Ava chirped a thank-you to Woodburn for finding her cell phone outside near the path to the lighthouse and told them they were welcome to come again, but she'd appreciate advance notice next time. Jessop lashed out with a snide comment. Woodburn said nothing until they reached the front door.

"If you see Liam Brody," he said to Ava, "call me immediately. Here's my card."

"Thank you," Ava said.

Liam pictured the tall, gray-haired marshal with his darting gaze and thick mustache. Woodburn offered kind advice. "Running away makes him seem guilty. If he contacts me, I can get him back on track for his trial."

"I'm not sure I understand," Ava said. "Would you cover up the fact that he ran?"

"I didn't say that."

"What exactly could you do for him?" she asked. "What can I tell him you'd do?"

"I'd be willing to testify about his cooperation. That way, his attorney can put a positive spin on the situation."

"Would he be able to remain out on bail?"

"Not a chance." His voice sounded definite. "Good night, Ms. Donovan."

The heavy front door slammed loudly. Woodburn had made Liam an offer, which he appreciated. Instead of tearing the lightkeeper's cottage apart in an intrusive search, Woodburn held out an olive branch. Liam had to wonder why. Did Woodburn know something he didn't?

Why didn't the marshal pursue a more diligent search? Had Ava threatened him with a lawsuit if he didn't provide her with a search warrant? Maybe Woodburn had come to the conclusion that he ought to return with a more effective investigative team than Deputy Jessop. Possibly, after a quick study of the cottage, the marshal decided they should concentrate on more promising leads. Liam had set a couple of false trails before he left Eugene. One pointed to a local airfield. Another went to the docks at Newport where he had a fleet of four boats, including a high-performance motorboat that could outrun most of the Coast Guard vessels and take him to Canada before a search got underway.

If fleeing from the area had been his goal, he had many options. But that wasn't the reason he came here. He wanted to stay and investigate, using the specialized knowledge that Ava knew from growing up in Narcissus. He heard her outside the passageway.

"They're gone," she said. "But there's no guarantee they won't be back. Meet me upstairs in my bedroom."

He'd been waiting for that invitation ever since they first

Fugitive Harbor

met, six years ago on his dive boat. But the context was all wrong. They wouldn't be sharing a bed. Not tonight.

AFTER SHE LEFT the den, Ava circled through the first floor, turning off the lights as she went from the study to the dining room to the kitchen and back to the entryway. Her path progressed slowly and deliberately, giving her time to calm down and gather her thoughts. Though she didn't want to give in to fear, the visit from the police had left her shaken.

And the approaching confrontation with Liam would be difficult. Though she cared about him and about seeing justice done, Woodburn's advice made her stop and reconsider. Harboring Liam was breaking the law. No two ways about it. And she didn't want to go to jail.

Though she'd thought of him many, many times during the past six years and he played a major role in her fantasy life, Ava didn't owe him anything. It was presumptuous of him to ask for her help, very demanding, very alpha male. Without warning, he'd strolled back into her life and upset her plans. The lighthouse project could be the taking off point for an interesting, lucrative career in historic renovations. Exactly the sort of thing she'd been hoping for. The smart thing would be to tell Liam to contact Woodburn and wish him luck at his trial.

But she didn't trust the justice system. Innocent people were convicted all the time. She remembered her brother, incarcerated for twelve years because the police failed to investigate thoroughly. How could she refuse to help Liam in the same situation? He needed her. And she was a sucker for reclamation projects, whether it meant feeding the runt in a litter of kittens with an eyedropper or performing a makeover on a friend for a special date.

She made her way to the carved staircase that ascended

from the entryway through the center of the house. Unlike the carvings on the front door, the oak balustrades and newel posts had been painted several different colors over the years. She'd have to research the history of the house before she stripped the paint and restained the original wood.

At the top of the staircase, she turned left on the landing. The primary bedroom—her room—boasted a worn armchair and table by the window along with other heavy oak furniture. Also, there was an attached bathroom with a claw-foot tub and, of course, the large walk-in closet where the secret passageway connected from the den downstairs. The glow from a small bedside lamp shed just enough light for her to notice Liam, standing by the window and holding the curtain aside so he could see out. The rain had begun to let up, and moonlight filtered past the edge of the curtain to outline his profile.

To help him or not to help him? That was one of many questions. Could she turn her back on someone who might be wrongly accused? Was she being a fool to accept Liam's amnesia alibi? Was her former professor, in truth, a killer?

He turned his head toward her and grinned. His dark eyebrows gave his face character while his sharp cheekbones and square chin provided structure. He'd taken off his rain jacket and rolled up the sleeves on the plaid shirt he wore over a long-sleeved thermal T-shirt. Tall and lean and sexy, he was the whole package. Not that she had any intention of unwrapping him.

"We need to talk," he said.

"Sounds like you're breaking up with me."

If so, she had the perfect breakup speech, starting with the classic: *It's not you. It's me.* She'd explain how she didn't want to get involved, didn't want to take a chance on blowing her reputation and losing this renovation project. As these arguments circulated in her head, she hated the cold, callous direction of her thinking. How had she turned into a person who valued her profession more than his freedom?

She climbed onto the queen bed with the four-poster frame and curled her legs up under her bottom. He took the arm-chair. "Okay, Liam. Talk."

"I put you in a lousy position. When I heard Jess-hole be-rating you and Woodburn posing his questions, I realized that it wasn't right for me to ask you to take this kind of risk. You hardly know me."

All true. "Actually, it'd be worse if you knew me better and took advantage."

"If I knew you well…" He flashed a rakish grin and arched his left eyebrow like a caricature of a rogue. "If I knew you in the biblical sense, we'd have some awesome memories."

"Awesome, huh?" She scoffed. "You might be overesti-mating your allure."

"Only telling the truth."

She glided her hand down a bedpost, ornately carved with delicate flowers. Though she hadn't meant for the gesture to be sexy, she felt the smooth, sanded texture of the wood beneath her fingers. His steady gaze lit a flame inside her. "What else did you want to say?"

"I'm proud of you, Ava." He cleared his throat and keyed his tone to sound more like a proper professor. "You're a top student, even if you didn't go into maritime archeology. You've built your research skills, worked tirelessly in the field and gained the respect of academics and others involved in the preservation of history. This restoration at Cape Ab-solute should place you at the forefront in your profession."

His compliments made her blush. "Have you been follow-ing my exploits in the alumni bulletins and on local news?"

"Damn right," he said. "I would have sent a congratulations bouquet when I heard about this lighthouse job, but the timing wasn't right. I was tied up with these pesky murder charges."

When she read about his arraignment, she'd wanted to offer her support and had been tempted to reach out. At the time, she'd had her own life to consider. Preparing to move here, finally abdicating her relationship with Portland Jimmy and gathering research materials took time and energy. *An excuse, and not a very good one.* While she'd been occupied with her hotshot career, Liam was drowning offshore. The least she could have done was throw him a life preserver.

"Anyway," he said, "I'll be moving on. No one needs to know I was here."

But I'll know. And she'd feel forever guilty. "At the very least, you need to stay for a couple of hours in case Jess-hole and Woodburn are watching the house."

He shook his head. "It won't take much for me to sneak into the forest and disappear."

Half of her brain screamed for her to let him go. But the other half was louder and would not be ignored. This time her decision was final.

"Stay," she whispered.

"Do you believe I'm innocent?"

"This isn't about you, Liam. It's about the truth." A shadow darkened her thoughts. If someone had helped her brother and investigated more thoroughly, the jury would never have sent him to jail.

Liam's voice was gentle. "What is it, Ava? What's wrong?"

"My middle brother, Michael was wrongly convicted of murder. If someone had listened to him earlier, he'd have twelve years of his life back. I'm doing this for him."

The stakes couldn't be higher. If she'd misjudged him and his claim of amnesia was a sham, Ava had just invited a cold-blooded killer into her life.

Chapter Five

"In the meantime…" Ava hopped off the bed and headed toward the closet "…we should get you settled in a safe place to spend the night."

"The lighthouse," he suggested.

"I've got a better idea." Elizabeth Mayes, the long-ago lightkeeper, would have approved. She loved the passageway, and Ava had improved it. "A secret within a secret."

Inside the bedroom closet, she rearranged her shoes in front of the secret passage entrance, noticing that two pairs had been shuffled. Had to be the work of Jess-hole, what a jerk. She opened the hatch, sliding the door aside and stepped over the neat row of shoes onto the ledge. Climbing down the crude ladder—thick boards nailed to vertical studs—required very little concentration though she was descending into darkness.

If she and Liam were going to bring this investigation to a successful close, they needed to get started right away. She considered how to proceed and decided the first order of business would be to get the lay of the land by talking to someone she trusted. Her sister, Rachel, worked part-time at the pharmacy adjoining the market and heard enough gossip to provide an accurate picture of how the folks in Narcissus viewed the murder of Stuart Whitcomb.

Rachel, only two years older than Ava, had followed in

their mother's footsteps by getting married when she was eighteen and popping out two wonderful, smart, healthy children before she was thirty. Rachel's greatest talent was baking. When upset or troubled, she retreated to the kitchen and got busy, whipping out breads, muffins, cakes and cookies. She claimed the activity settled her mind and gave her focus. Nobody in the family contradicted, mainly because they couldn't talk with their mouths full of the delectable sweetness she created.

Ava had a similar habit. Instead of cooking, she built stuff. At age four, she constructed an elaborate, three-story dollhouse. During the summer after first grade, she built a clubhouse from scrap wood. With a sheet of plastic over the window and a door that opened and closed, she sanded, swept and decorated using a leftover paint from projects around the house. The end result was too cool. Her three obnoxious brothers begged to be let in, and she complied. *Big mistake!* They took over.

While she climbed down the crude ladder in the secret passageway, she told Liam about her construction efforts. "The best," she said, "was in third grade. I built a tree house in the giant hemlock at the edge of our property. Heavy work and complicated, but I didn't ask my dork-face brothers for help. This new, improved clubhouse would be No Boys Allowed."

"Sounds fair to me." His deep voice echoed in the passageway. "You did the work, so you deserved the privacy."

"A tree house is easier to defend. I gathered a bunch of pinecones and pelted the dorks whenever they tried to climb inside."

"You were a tough little third grader."

"Better believe it."

On the first floor, she waited for him to step down beside

her with his pocket-size flashlight showing the way. In the five-by-six-foot rectangle, they were forced to stand within inches of each other. The natural heat from his body radiated toward her, and his jeans—still damp from the rain—moistened her flannel pajamas. Too easily, she imagined their legs entwined as the distance between them vanished. She could almost feel the hard planes of his chest and the sheltering strength in his arms.

Without meeting his gaze, she took the flashlight from his hand, ignoring the sizzle when their skin touched. She inched toward her left until she reached a wall of unvarnished siding, made up of eighteen-inch-wide boards. At the farthest edge, hidden by shadows, she found a small handhold and pulled. The wall folded on invisible hinges like an accordion. "Ta-da," she said. "It's a secret room within a secret passageway."

He murmured, "No boys allowed."

"Well, you're welcome to come in." She tugged on a dangling cord, and a bare 75-watt bulb came to life.

"Did you build this secret hideout?"

"Actually, no. Someone else put it together, but I found it and made a few repairs, mostly just oiling the hardware. It only took a couple of hours."

The ceiling in the secret room was as tall as the study. Liam could stand without bumping his head. In other ways, the dimensions matched the typical size of a prison cell: six-by-eight feet. She used the space to store her camping equipment, including sleeping bags, a couple of tents, a lantern, a Coleman stove and tarps that smelled faintly of old campfires. Never had she considered using this stuffy, little area as a guest room. But she enjoyed the idea of having a secret place inside the lightkeeper's historic cottage.

"Electricity," he said, looking up at the bulb. "That could come in handy."

"Is there something you want to plug in?"

"My laptop."

She raised her eyebrows. "I don't see a computer."

"I left it in the lighthouse," he said, "before I tipped over the ladder."

This was a story she wanted to hear. What was he doing with the ladder? She spread one of the sleeping bags on the dusty wood floor and sat. "I'm going to need more explanation."

"When I got here, I had second thoughts about coming inside and putting you in jeopardy. Especially in the middle of the night." He folded his long legs and sat beside her. "I had a plan. I figured I could stay in the lighthouse until dawn."

Not a clever move. "What made you think nobody would look for a runaway fugitive in a forty-eight-foot-tall tower? The lighthouse doesn't exactly fade into the background."

"I said that I had a plan. Not necessarily a *good* plan."

"Then what?"

"I set the ladder so I could climb up and look in one of the windows."

"Let me get this straight," she said. "You decided to use an aluminum ladder during a lightning storm."

"I took my chances. When I looked inside I saw how badly the stairs were damaged. There's a large section—probably four feet—torn away from the wall. There's no way to reach the top floor of the lighthouse until repairs are made." He gave a self-deprecating shrug. "That was when I came up with another idea. I tucked my backpack—holding my computer, clothes, a couple of burner phones and other supplies—into a dark corner of the busted stairs."

"When you were climbing down," she concluded for him, "you tipped the ladder over."

"I should go out and get my backpack."

For a long moment, they sat quietly. Outdoors, the thunder continued to roar and the heavy rain thrummed against the windows. Farther away on the road or in the forest, there might be officers watching for a sign that Liam was here. "I don't think you should risk going out there tonight. Apart from the danger of a lightning strike, it's too easy for Woodburn to set up surveillance. What do you need your computer for?"

"I've made notes on my investigation into Stuart's murder."

"That would be helpful in planning our next step. I'm scheduled to see Georgina tomorrow and might get a chance to talk to her creepy husband."

"Tomorrow? But it's Sunday."

"The one day of the week when I don't have workers scheduled. Sunday afternoon is a great time to see Georgina. Plus I want to talk to my sister who happens to be friends with Holly Louise, Stuart's ex-wife."

"Holly is on my suspect list. She and her son, Oliver, will both inherit access to what's left of his fortune."

Ava stood and turned toward the door. "I'll get my laptop. You can access your files on the cloud. Is that possible? If so, can other investigators trace your progress?"

"Yes, you can access. No, others can't. I'm not a computer genius, but I'm pretty good. My data is secure."

"Good."

Before she left the secret room, he caught her hand. She looked down into his silver-gray eyes. He whispered, "Thank you."

"You're going to owe me big-time for helping you get ac-
quitted."

"I won't forget."

And if he wasn't innocent, she hoped he wouldn't blame
her for failing him.

GRATEFUL THAT HE didn't suffer from claustrophobia, Liam
spread out a second sleeping bag opposite hers and created a
sort of table from a couple of cardboard boxes with "Camp"
scrawled on the side with marker. His gaze bounced off the
rough wood walls. The secret room was too small, grungy
and stuffy to be comfortable; however, for the first time since
he discovered Stuart's body and started CPR, he felt safe.
Finally, he had someone on his side. His breathing settled
into an easy rhythm, and his tension relaxed enough for him
to turn his head without hearing the pops and crackles of
knotted muscles across his neck and shoulders. Thanks to
Ava, he might get through this trial.

When she returned, her arms were full. In addition to the
laptop, she brought a thermos—which he hoped was filled
with coffee—a six-pack of water, her phone and a reusable
grocery bag holding paper plates and snacks. She set him
up with pita chips, an apple and a container of roasted red
pepper hummus, all of which he scarfed down.

"Hungry?" she asked wryly.

"A twelve-mile dash through the forest burns a lot of cal-
ories." He was usually in better physical condition. Not only
did he scuba dive a couple of times a week but he jogged
nearly every morning. The GPS ankle bracelet had curtailed
his outdoor workouts, limiting him to running on a tread-
mill and a couple of daily sessions on his ergometer rowing
machine that he called "the erg."

She handed over her computer. "You can get started. I'll make you something more substantial to eat."

He would have told her not to go to any special trouble, but that ship had left the marina. He'd already thrown her life into chaos, and he didn't expect the situation to get less complicated. In minutes, he accessed his data on her laptop and opened a file named "Holly Louise and Oliver."

When it came to renovation and home construction, Liam doubted he was as talented as Ava, but he sure as hell knew his way around electronics. Among the devices he carried in his backpack were bugs for listening and for tracking. He'd also rewired earbuds to make a portable, invisible walkie-talkie, something that would come in handy when they were working together and he couldn't show himself.

She slipped back into the secret room and passed him a plate containing a ham, tomato and cheese sandwich on a ciabatta roll. In her other hand, she held a steaming bowl of chili.

"Microwaved," she informed him. "I have plenty of food in the pantry and the freezer. My brother Jerome and a two-man crew have been working here all week, and they've got to eat."

"Does Jerome know about the secret passage?"

"No boys allowed," she reminded him of her motto. "This is *my* secret. No doubt, he'll eventually find out. But I like having a place where I can disappear."

"The guys in his crew, are they from Narcissus?"

She nodded. "Josh Ableman and Fish Finley. I think his real name is Edward, but everybody calls him Fish because of the 'fin' in 'Finley.'"

"I know him." Fish Finley worked part-time for him at Deep Dive. Until recently, Liam thought he and Fish were friends. "He's scheduled to testify at trial. Supposedly, Fish overheard an argument I had with Stuart."

"Yikes! Is there anybody in Narcissus who isn't involved in this murder?"

"Small town." He took a bite of the sandwich and chewed. *Delicious.* During these weeks at home with his anklet and little human contact, food had tasted like sawdust, and the aroma made him sick. Depressed? Maybe. He'd lost weight. One taste of Ava's sandwich and chili energized his will to live.

"Tomorrow," she said, "my first stop will be at Rachel's house. She always has a potluck starting at one. My regular meeting time with Georgina is at four."

"I want to be able to listen in. Also to communicate with you while you're talking."

"Not sure how you can pull that off. You're too big to be a fly on the wall."

"I have a few ideas."

"Maybe I can record the conversations on my phone. I've done that before when a client like Georgina comes up with detailed instructions I need to get exactly right."

"I have a walkie-talkie device. It's just an earbud and a tiny microphone. The problem is that we need to be within a hundred yards of each other for it to work."

"Which means you'd have to ride along with me." She thought for a moment, then said, "I can manage that. There's a huge toolbox in the back of my truck. Maybe a bit too short for your legs, you'll be cramped. And you'll feel every bump in the road."

"That's fine." Grateful for every bit of help, he had no room to complain. He dug into the homemade chili, savored the beef and beans and exhaled a sigh of sheer contentment. "All I need now is my backpack."

She took her phone from her pocket. "I'll check the weather app to find out when the rain is going to stop."

He smiled to himself. Following the weather was second nature to most Oregonians, ranging from farmers to skiers, to those who made their living from the sea like him. His salvage business took rain and wind into account before and during most of their dives. Though not totally accurate, especially when trying to guess a few days in advance, the predictions were mostly right on target. "I don't mind the storm. I can go out right now if you give me a key to the lighthouse door."

"What if somebody's watching?"

"I'll run."

She exhaled in a huff. "You really aren't good at planning, are you? According to my app, the storm is going to let up in forty-four minutes. We'll wait. Then I'll go to the lighthouse. Alone."

"How will you know where my backpack is hidden?"

"I'll figure it out."

No way would he let her take all the risk. If he got caught on the way to the lighthouse, she still had plausible deniability and could say she hadn't seen him. He finished off the sandwich and turned the laptop so she could see the screen. "This is what I've got so far about Holly Louise and Oliver."

She scrolled through the document. "Neatly organized. You start with factual data about the individual, the next section details their connection to the crime and finally you have your theories about possible motivations."

"I'm not a detective, but this investigation seems like another research project. I've added details that won't prove relevant. Better to have too much than not enough."

"Are you kidding with this motivational theory for Holly

Louise?" She pointed at the screen. "Alien or ghost intervention."

"You've lived in Oregon long enough to recognize the indigenous wackiness. Consider the motto for our largest city, Keep Portland Weird. Holly Louise might believe she was directed to kill her ex-husband by otherworldly sources. I've heard that she's a big fan of horoscopes, psychics and crystals."

"True. She has a bracelet made entirely from blue and gray agates she gathered herself. It's supposed to ground her and bring good fortune."

"Yet, she still married Stuart."

"My sister chalks that up to teenage hormones. Holly was only eighteen and pregnant when they tied the knot."

"I never knew."

"Not surprised," she said. "Guys don't tend to talk much about their relationships, not even to their business partners."

"Definitely the case with me and Stuart. We hardly ever talked about personal stuff." He finished the chili and considered licking the bowl before he politely set it down beside his makeshift table. "His son, Oliver, is seventeen. Old enough to have formed his own opinions about his father."

"Old enough to commit murder," she said.

"That theory had occurred to me. Oliver is an experienced diver."

She cocked her head to one side. "Are you thinking the murderer is a scuba diver who came aboard after you were unconscious?"

"Only a theory." If Oliver came onto the boat, it meant he'd already made a plan with his father. Stuart would have administered the knockout drug to Liam. Father and son were working together. But why? Why would the young man have drugged Liam and tried to pin the murder on him?

And why would Stuart plan his own murder? "I don't even know the kid."

"Neither do I," Ava admitted. "But my sister can fill in some of the blanks. Can you show me some of your other profiles?"

He shuffled through the computer screens. In addition to Holly Louise and Oliver Whitcomb, he'd listed Georgina Solomon Quincy along with her husband. He had files for Serena Whitcomb, Stuart's sister, and Charles Tancredo, the harbormaster at the Port of Newport. He managed both the commercial docks and the recreational marina. Tancredo claimed that Stuart owed him a quarter million dollars.

Ava pointed out a wide omission. "What about his parents?"

"His dad lives in Hawaii with his second wife. A neat alibi, plus he's filthy rich. Same for his mother, a Realtor who invested brilliantly. Serena, on the other hand, has blown through a lot of her inheritance."

"I'll talk to Rachel about her." Ava checked the time on her phone and gracefully rose to her feet. "It's just after two in the morning. I'm going to change clothes and dash out to the lighthouse. Might be good if you came out of hiding and kept an eye on things in the cottage. Stay away from windows so nobody can see you."

He followed her out of the secret passage to the foot of the staircase and watched the athletic sway of her hips as she jogged up the stairs. He went from room to room downstairs, avoiding windows, but when he cautiously peeked out, he saw that the weather forecast had been correct. The rain had ended, and the half-moon peeked out from behind a cloud.

Moonlight shone against the white lighthouse tower making the wear and tear of many years seem irrelevant. Though the beacon hadn't been activated for over fifty years, the tower stood as a symbol of safe passage. He hoped his journey would lead to a verdict of not guilty. Then he'd be free to tell Ava the truth about his feelings for her.

Chapter Six

"Don't follow me." In the enclosed back porch behind the kitchen, Ava stuck her arms into a hooded, lavender rain jacket that draped long enough to cover her bottom. She slipped her phone in the pocket. "If you see anyone approach me on my way to the lighthouse, go back to the secret passage, lock yourself in and wait for me to come back."

"You're the boss," he drawled.

"That's right. I am."

She figured Liam to be one of those guys who saw himself as the skipper rather than the deckhand who saluted, followed orders and said, Aye, captain. *Too bad for him.* She had to be in charge, couldn't take the risk of having Jess-hole or the marshal come back and arrest her. She had to summon all her confidence and give orders like she meant them. From her years working construction with her brother, she knew how to act like a boss.

The overhead kitchen light outlined his shoulders and streaked through his thick, dark hair while he drank another cup of coffee. She resisted the urge to order him to lay off the caffeine or he'd never get to sleep. Maybe he was one of those odd people who could have coffee right before bed. In any case, she was a boss. Not his mommy.

She cleared her throat. "Does it bother you to have a woman tell you what to do?"

"I expect nothing less from you." Though respectful enough, she heard a touch of irony as he continued, "When I came to you, I didn't expect to find a nervous, little dormouse. I like a woman who takes charge."

"Word of advice," she said, "that's enough coffee."

Wearing her rain-resistant jacket, a thermal shirt, jeans and waterproof boots, she felt a hundred times more prepared than during her last mad dash to the lighthouse tower. The rain had slowed to a drizzle, and the cloudy skies—unmarred by lightning—painted the rocks and forests with a pale blue serenity. After she descended the back stairs to the yard carrying the Maglite, she glanced over her shoulder toward the kitchen door. She couldn't see Liam, which was a good thing. He knew better than to stand at a window where someone could see him.

The misty air outside the house brushed her cheeks. Chilly but not cold, the night refreshed her almost as much as reviewing the information Liam had put together. He'd compared his investigation to a research project, and she agreed. They'd work well together.

She moved quickly across the fifty yards separating the cottage from the lighthouse. The half-moon and stars lit her path, making the flashlight unnecessary. She turned it off. Though she doubted any law enforcement officers had been assigned to watch the cottage and surrounding properties all night, she'd rather not call attention to herself by waving a Maglite through the darkness.

At the outer entrance, she unlocked the lighthouse door and pushed it open. Moonlight spilled through the two high windows, creating shadows against the dirty white walls and splotches of naked brick where the plaster had peeled away. A six-foot mound of scrap wood piled up beside the door. Ava had tried to clear away the broken furniture and the damaged stairs that formerly clung to the circular wall and climbed to the room at the top where the beacon had been housed a long time ago.

Using the flashlight beam, she studied the damaged staircase. The first four steps on the bottom were intact but the railing was gone. Theoretically, the risers were usable, but so shaky she hardly dared put her weight on them. After more broken stairs came the long break where the staircase had been completely torn away, which was about four feet long. She estimated that the semi-intact lower stairs rose twenty-seven inches, followed by damaged stairs leading to four feet of empty space. The first solidly anchored stair was almost ten feet from the floor. That riser was bolted to the wall. When she was ready to start work on the staircase, she'd reach the upper stairs with a ladder. For now, climbing was unsafe.

She aimed the flashlight beam higher and spotted Liam's black backpack tucked into a corner of a higher stair directly below the window, approximately fifteen feet off the floor. Reaching it wouldn't be easy. She needed something long to extend her grasp. Since she'd been using the lighthouse to store carpentry equipment and yard implements, she had options. Poking through the tools, she discovered a bow rake with tines she could use to hook the straps on the backpack… if she could reach it.

Getting into position below the stairs, she extended the rake as far as she could, still coming up short. She wished for an additional six inches in height. There had to be something in here that she could stand on.

She heard the door open. Liam whispered, "Deputy Jessop is hammering at the front door of the cottage."

She'd been so focused on the immediate problem of snagging the backpack straps that it took a moment to comprehend what he was saying. "Why is he here?"

"Didn't think I ought to ask." He took the rake from her. "Go out there and talk to him."

"What about you?"

"I'll figure something out."

"We should have done this your way. If I'd stayed in the cottage, I could have answered the door and gotten rid of—"

"Just go."

She dodged around the junk inside the lighthouse and went out the door. In the moonlight, she saw Jessop charging around the side of the house with a flashlight in one hand and a gun in the other. She and her brothers made fun of the mean-spirited deputy, but she knew he had a vicious temper. *Jessop was no laughing matter.* Once, he'd beaten Barry into unconsciousness. Only a few hours ago, he'd slapped a handcuff on her wrist, twisted her arm and aimed his weapon at her. If Woodburn hadn't been there to rein Jessop in, that situation could have gotten real messy real fast.

Now Jessop was back. Alone.

Her confidence evaporated, leaving her vulnerable. Somehow she had to convince him that she had nothing to hide and he shouldn't enter the lighthouse. If he found Liam, he'd probably shoot both of them. She raised her trembling hand and waved to him. "Over here, Deputy."

He halted and braced the pistol in a straight-armed, one-handed stance while still holding his flashlight with the other. "Stand still. Show me your hands, girl. Don't move."

She did as he ordered, being careful not to provoke him. Keeping her voice gentle and nonthreatening, she said, "Let's go inside. I'll make herbal tea, and I think I have some leftover marionberry pie that I can heat up."

"I'm not here for a damn snack. I'm here to apprehend your damn boyfriend."

"Who?"

"The fugitive, Liam Brody."

Her mouth went dry. It took all her restraint to keep from looking over her shoulder at the lighthouse. "I don't know what to tell you, Deputy. You and Marshal Woodburn already searched everywhere."

"You're up to something. Don't tell me you're not."

Jessop came closer, stopping when only three feet away from her. Still holding his gun, he swept the flashlight beam from the top of her head to the tips of her toes. The light lingered on her breasts, and he stared hard. But she didn't move, didn't flinch. *Don't do anything to make him angrier.* "Please, let's go inside the cottage."

"You're in a heap of trouble," he said as he turned off the flashlight and slipped it into a holder on his utility belt. "What the hell are you doing out here?"

"I had to check on something in the lighthouse." She kept herself from saying too much. The more she elaborated on an excuse, the more ways he could trip her up.

"How come?"

"I need to make sure the report on my progress is accurate. Tomorrow, I meet with my employer, Georgina Solomon Quincy." She emphasized the name, hoping to impress Jessop. Everybody in Lincoln County knew of the wealthy Solomon family.

"Miss Georgina is friends with Stuart's family. You know how those rich people stick together. And I'm damn sure she'll be angry when she finds out that you're harboring his killer."

"I'm sure you're right, Deputy." She knew for a fact that he was dead wrong. Georgina despised Stuart, his ex-wife, his mother and his sister. But Ava knew better than to contradict Jessop. Her brothers had taught her to never poke a skunk. Cowards were most dangerous when proven wrong. "Is it all right for me to put my hands down?"

"Not yet." He thrust the pistol toward her. "I'm stiff and tired, and it's all your fault."

"Sorry," she murmured. *Don't contradict him.*

"I've been parked in the forest, watching and waiting after Woodburn took off to search in other places. I saw lights come on in your bedroom and your kitchen. Don't you ever sleep?"

"My nerves are on edge. I don't usually get visits from the police in the middle of the night."

"Don't lie to me." He barked a harsh laugh. "Plenty of times I showed up on the Donovan doorstep to arrest Barry in the middle of the night after the bars closed. And don't get me started on Michael. I'll never believe that punk is innocent."

Her jaw clenched. Anger sliced through her fear as she instinctively reacted to his cruel comment about her unjustly accused brother. She took back a sliver of her self-control. "How can I help you?"

"I want to see inside the damn lighthouse. Use your key to open the door." He gestured with the gun. "Come on, let's go."

"You were already in there."

"Do what I say. I'm not going to ask politely again." He took another step closer and shoved her shoulder, throwing her off balance. She caught herself before falling. He shoved again. "Do I need the cuffs? Maybe you like being restrained. Do you like it when your boyfriend ties you up?"

Disgusted and outraged, she pulled her phone from her pocket. "I'm recording this conversation. Starting now."

"What the hell?"

"I need a record of what you're saying to use in court. I might sue the sheriff's office for police harassment. Touch me again, and the charge goes up to police brutality."

His thin lips curled in a sneer. "Bitch."

"Speak up, Deputy Jessop. I didn't catch that word."

"No more games, little girl. I want to look inside the lighthouse. A reasonable request." Still holding his gun at the ready, he strode past her toward the door. "I'm an officer of the law, just doing my damn duty."

She wanted to shout at him, but panic choked her words. If the deputy walked inside, he'd find Liam. "Wait! You don't have a warrant."

"Well, look here." His long nose twitched as if catching the scent of his prey. "The door isn't locked, and I hear sounds of a fight going on inside."

"That's a lie. Nobody is in there."

"Not the way I see it. I need to investigate."

When he grasped the doorknob, she felt her life crumbling. All her years of study and hard work would be wiped away. She'd have a criminal record. No one would ever hire her to do another historic renovation.

Jessop shoved the door open and burst inside, holding his pistol with both hands. Triumphantly, he shouted, "I've got you now."

Frozen in place, she looked to the skies, seeking solace in the stars and the moon. *No regrets.* Even if she went to jail, she knew that helping Liam had been the right decision. She believed him innocent, unjustly prosecuted for a murder he didn't commit, and he had no one else on his side. *Sometimes, you just have to do what you think is right and accept the consequences.*

Her gaze was caught by a flash from the beacon room at the top of the lighthouse. Concentrating hard, she saw a glimmer of light from one of the windows. It drew a circle on the glass, then paused, then drew a circle again. Sometimes on scuba expeditions at night in dark seas, they used flashlight signals to communicate. Drawing a circle with a light was code for "everything is okay." Somehow, Liam had made it to the top of the tower, and he was letting her know he was all right, using his powerful pocket Maglite.

From inside the lighthouse, she heard Jessop yelling. "Son of a bitch! Where the hell are you?"

She exhaled in a gush, unaware of holding her breath. Her pulse rate steadied as energy flowed back into her body. She had no idea how Liam had managed to reach the upper floor of the lighthouse tower. *Sprouted wings and flew to the rafters?* It felt like a miracle—a sign that she was supposed to be working with him.

With her feet braced in a solid stance, she raised her phone to record Jess-hole when he emerged from the lighthouse. "Well, Deputy, what do you have to say for yourself?"

His eyebrows lowered, and his chin stuck out. In spite of the chilly night air, his forehead dripped with sweat. She'd won this round, and her victory felt good.

He rushed toward her. When close enough, he slapped the phone from her hand into the mud. "You're not going to get away with this."

She squatted down, picked up her phone and brushed off the mud, impressed that the screen was still lit. "Second time today," she muttered. "I just finished cleaning this thing off."

"I'm not giving up. I'm going to watch you and follow you until that fugitive is caught and you both go to jail."

When she looked up and saw the hatred in his eyes, Ava couldn't help being scared. Bravely, she stood up to him. "Is that supposed to be a threat?"

"A promise, Ms. Donovan."

When he pivoted and stalked away from her, she saw cruel determination in the rigid set of his shoulders. Deputy Jessop meant what he'd said.

Chapter Seven

Looking down from the windows in the circular room at the top of the lighthouse, Liam watched Jessop stomp around the cottage to where he'd parked his black SUV with the Lincoln County Sheriff's Department logo. Walking at a fast and furious pace, the deputy looked like the definition of a frustrated, angry man—a guy who wanted to kick butt and take names but didn't have a pencil.

Liam shifted his focus to Ava, who stood frozen between the cottage and the lighthouse in the exact same place she'd faced Jessop. The light purple hood on her jacket had fallen back, and the wind ruffled her dark, curly, chin-length hair. Her arms wrapped around her middle as if holding herself together. She was too far away for him to see if she was shaking with fear or to hear a tremble in her voice, but he'd seen Jessop knock her phone from her hand and snarl. She didn't deserve this kind of bullying from the law. Nobody did.

Using one of the burner phones he had stored in his backpack, he sent her a text. Come to the tower. Pretend you're locking up but come inside.

He saw her wipe the screen on her cell phone, nod once and take a shaky step toward the lighthouse. Meanwhile, Jessop had slammed the door of his SUV and driven away. Liam watched the red taillights disappear into the forest. This time, the departure was real. The deputy wasn't hanging around. Once again, Liam had escaped discovery.

Earlier tonight, he wasn't sure he'd make it, but he'd found a way. When he reached the room at the top, he'd discovered that other people had been here before him. They'd left a couple of sleeping bags and a long, double-strand rope with thick knots every eighteen inches to use for climbing. Anchored to the pedestal for the beacon, the rope felt like a solid support. He opened the hatch and tossed it through, pleased to see that it almost touched the floor, nearly forty-two feet below.

He lowered himself onto the rope and descended, grateful for the upper body strength he'd developed during the weeks he'd spent confined to his house. Twice-daily workouts on the erg had paid off big-time as he gripped the rope and used his legs and feet to balance on the knots. About five feet from the floor, he let go and dropped. Ava awaited.

Before he could explain and apologize, she set her flashlight down on the floor. With her hands free, she joined her body with his. Her arms wrapped around his neck, and she buried her face against his chest. Not weeping but breathing heavily, she clung to him with fierce strength as though he were her lifeline—the only thing keeping her from floating into the night sky like a lost balloon.

Her words trickled out between gasps. "I thought we were caught. Going to jail. No way out. Can't believe it. Jessop outsmarted me."

He caressed her shoulders and slid his hands lower to her slender waist. "He's not clever enough to beat us. Luckier than he has any right to be. And as stubborn as a hungry honey badger. That makes him dangerous."

"Yes," she whispered, "he won't give up."

"Neither will we." The fragrance of her shampoo reminded him of lilacs in the spring. "There are two of us. We're tough, and we smell good."

"What?"

"You and me. Champions of the world."

She tilted her head and gazed up at him. Moonlight from the high windows glistened on her cheeks and sparkled in her blue eyes. She cleared her throat. When she spoke, her voice was calm. "You changed clothes."

"I had other stuff in my backpack. I needed to get out of the wet jeans."

"Where did you find the fancy rope?"

"Ava, we don't have time to talk. I watched Jessop drive away, but he might come back or send someone else for a stakeout."

She bobbed her head. "The rope?"

"I found it in the room at the top. Somebody else must have been here."

"That room is called the lantern room. Above is a metal dome or cupola with an air vent and lightning rod on top. And the stairs…" She paused her lecture to gaze at the snaggle-toothed spiral staircase with impossibly large gaps. "How did you get up there?"

"Free climbing," he said, again pleased about his rowing muscles. "I jumped up to grab the lowest stair that was still attached to the brick wall. Twisting and turning, I maneuvered from stair to stair. When the boards creaked and buckled under my weight, I supported myself with my arms. And vice versa. Not a trip I want to make again."

"When I saw you make the sign for okay in the window, I almost fainted from relief." The tiniest hint of a smile touched her lips. "Before that, I was almost too scared to breathe. I thought Jessop was going to shoot both of us."

"If you've changed your mind about helping me and want

to end this collaboration, I can live with that. When I saw Jessop pushing you around, I regretted being here and wanted to kill the son of a bitch."

"Don't say things like that. When you talk about murder, it makes me doubt the wisdom of playing on Team Liam."

In spite of his need to get moving and seek a safe haven, her nearness calmed him. He whispered, "I'm sorry."

She reached up and held his face in her hands. "Earlier, I agreed to help you. But now… I'm committed. I believe in you, maybe more than you believe in yourself."

Rising up on her tiptoes, she confirmed her words with a light kiss. The softness of her lips wakened his strength and his determination. He pulled her close, savoring the delicate pressure of her pliant body against his chest. He kissed her back, tender at first and then with rising passion. The taste of her sweet, warm mouth drew him deeper. His tongue probed between her lips, gliding across the slick surface of her teeth and then went deeper. A growl vibrated in his throat. He wanted more of her, wanted everything from her.

But he wouldn't take advantage. Yes, she'd kissed him. But would she agree to more? "The view from the lantern room is magic. The topmost branches of Sitka spruce waving in the wind. Moonlight shimmering. Breakers churning."

She inhaled a ragged gasp. "Captains on passing ships reported they could see the lantern's beam from twenty-three miles out, and I expect the same is true in reverse."

"Ava, will you stay here with me tonight? In the lighthouse."

Though he expected a no, she didn't immediately turn him down. Instead, she stepped away from his embrace and eyed the knotted rope. "I'm not quite ready to make that climb."

"I'll help."

"I bet you will." She gave a light chuckle. "Might be easier if you came back to the cottage with me."

Every bone, muscle and nerve in his body urged him to say yes. His arms felt empty when he wasn't holding her. She was perfect. He wanted to make love to her. But he couldn't risk it. "Tonight I stay here."

"You're sure?"

"Being here is strategic."

"How so?"

"If Jessop or anybody else finds me, you can claim that you didn't know I was there."

She tensed. "You want me to lie?"

"In the service of a greater truth," he said. "When you go, leave the lighthouse door unlocked. Tomorrow morning, I'll sneak into the barn. When you're ready to make the drive to your sister's house, back your truck in there, and I'll hide in the truck bed."

"Better idea," she said. "I already have a Hyundai Sonata parked in the barn. Excellent space in the trunk and the back seats fold down so you could crawl through."

Whether he curled up in the trunk or in the bed of her truck, the drive to Narcissus wouldn't be a pleasure cruise. "I'm guessing the Sonata has a better ride than the truck."

"Not nearly as bone jarring." She took a set of keys from her pocket, detached a key fob with the curvy Hyundai logo and handed it to him. "Can I call you?"

"Calls and texts should be okay." He waved his cell phone. "This is a burner."

She reminded him, "Woodburn was able to trace you the first time you called me on a burner phone."

"I think he overheard my part of our conversation on a bug planted in the house. Not by tracking the phone. Besides, I have a better idea." He reached into a jacket pocket and pulled out a small case. "Practice wearing these earbuds. And try different ways of fastening the microphone to your clothes so you can talk back to me."

"This is like something a spy would use. For espionage."

"Just remember. We're the good guys, and the good guys always win."

In the movies. No matter what peril they faced, the sultry heroine and dashing hero would triumph. He hoped, for once, real life would follow that script.

LATER THAT NIGHT, Liam stretched out on the sleeping bags and blankets of his makeshift bed in the lantern room at the top of the lighthouse. His muscles ached from the incredibly long day of running, climbing and hiding. His physical stress couldn't compare to the way his emotions battered his mind. Worse than the fear and rage he felt for himself were his feelings for Ava. An incredible woman, she was strong and beautiful, and he wanted to know her better. At the same time, he regretted coming here and putting her in danger. He didn't deserve her attention when he couldn't even promise that he hadn't killed Stuart. His guilt if anything happened would be overwhelming.

Ironically, he was the only witness to the murder. Somehow, he had to remember. The therapist he'd hired to help him recall his memories had suggested a form of focused meditation when he went to bed. With eyes closed, Liam concentrated on sensations he experienced before losing consciousness on the boat. Sprawled on the cushions in the stern lounging area, he'd felt the heat of the afternoon sun and the spray from the twin motors. Stuart had been trying to convince him to purchase this cabin cruiser for the Deep Dive fleet, but Liam had disagreed. This was a luxury yacht. Too fancy.

Gradually, he emptied his mind of all other thought. Stuart's voice faded into a blend of noise from circling gulls and splashing waves. Liam kept his eyes closed, regulated his breathing and waited for his indistinct memories to take solid form. His thoughts were uncensored, fanciful. As he often did, he imagined a mermaid perched on a rock, singing softly and combing her long, brown hair. Then came a deep, soft stillness.

This was new. Liam forced himself not to waken and break the spell of imagination and memory. He heard the sound of an outboard motor and knew another boat was approaching. Though he didn't move or rouse himself, he could see it in his mind's eye. An inflatable like a Zodiac. He recognized the sounds of the inflatable hooking up to the dive platform where the twin motors rested in silence. Another person was coming aboard.

Liam's pulse raced. His muscles tensed. Finally, he would see the murderer.

Anticipation heightened his senses. The moment blasted his meditative state. He returned to reality. Too soon.

He bolted to his feet. Shattered bits of memory scattered around his feet as he made his way to the windows looking out to sea. Out there, the answers were hidden. Someone else, not necessarily a scuba diver, had been on the yacht with him and Stuart. Was that mystery person the killer?

THE NEXT MORNING at about eight o'clock, Ava put the finishing touches on a huge breakfast of bagels, smoked salmon, cream cheese, sausage and omelet which she packed in a basket. Also included were bottles of water, juice, energy bars, a thermos filled with coffee and other supplies Liam had requested. When she stepped outside, she blinked at the welcome burst of sunshine. On a day like this, it was hard to imagine murder and danger. She paused at the starting point of a steep path that descended to the narrow, sandy beach. Offshore were dramatic rock formations resulting from lava flows fifteen million years ago.

The three largest basalt formations, called the "sea hags" because they resembled giant silhouettes of stooped figures wearing ragged robes, were home to raucous colonies of nesting seabirds. Cormorants, gulls and white-chested murres competed for territory on the sea hags guarding the tide pools. Seal Rock provided a long, flat surface at the edge of the breaking surf for marine mammals who were already sunning themselves on this fine, clear April day.

Ava moved on. She inhaled a breath of salty air and hummed as she approached the tower. The mic and earbuds had been working beautifully, and she used the device to let him know she'd arrived. "Lower the rope, Rapunzel."

"Don't compare me to a fairy-tale princess."

She chuckled. "If the glass slipper fits..."

"And what does that make you?"

"Obviously, I'm the fairy godmother."

The knotted rope slithered down from the lantern room. She tied it to the basket handle, and he pulled the food and supplies up to his lair. Though he was close enough to hear her if she shouted, Ava had gotten accustomed to the unexpected intimacy from their wireless walkie-talkie. In a normal tone of voice, she asked, "I understand why you need binoculars, but why the hammer and screwdriver?"

"To repair the latch on the door to the lantern room and also on this hatch." He hauled the basket inside. "Mmm, coffee. Maybe you are a fairy godmother, after all."

"I texted my sister first thing this morning. Departure time is one fifteen."

"I'll be waiting in the barn."

She imagined him checking his Casio G-Shock dive watch and making a mental note with a quick nod of his head. Her memories of her former professor—and her slight obsession with him when she was a student—became more clearly defined as they spent more time together. Liam hadn't physically changed much from six years ago, still lean and muscular. Maybe his biceps were bigger. It was hard to tell without seeing him shirtless.

As she strolled away from the lighthouse and went to the cottage, her memory replayed a day when she and the rest of her class were on Liam's boat, changing into wet suits. While he gave instructions for the tactical dive, she'd been stealing glances at his tanned upper body and muscular arms. He looked healthy, exactly the way a man should look. Not too heavily muscled. Definitely not too skinny.

And now, finally, she'd kissed him for real. Last night was different from that shy, long-ago kiss on the boat. Last night had been passionate. Tender at first, then quickly progressing to ferocious. She'd felt how excited he was and how much he wanted her. His desire had little to do with their investigation and everything to do with untamed, unbridled lust of a man for a woman. *Wishful thinking?* She entered the cottage through the back door, stepped into the kitchen and sank into a chair at the table.

Her first priority was to get control of her imagination before she saw Rachel. Her sister had always been able to read her emotions, which was why she'd texted a couple of messages about dropping by for a visit rather than calling and betraying the urgency in her tone.

If Ava turned bright red and stammered every time Liam's name was mentioned, their association would be revealed. The best way for her to control a difficult situation had always meant intense organization. She prepared lunch for Liam and made cherry and macadamia nut cookies to take to Rachel's. Considering her sister's baking obsession, bringing baked goods was like carrying snow to a polar bear or chocolate to Hershey, Pennsylvania.

With less than an hour to go before departure time, she sat at the rolltop desk and reviewed Liam's notes on her laptop, trying to decide what sort of questions she ought to ask her sister. Mainly, she'd focus on Stuart's ex-wife. How much did Holly Louise Whitcomb inherit after her husband's death? And what about her son, Oliver?

According to Liam's notes, Holly had an unshakable alibi—an Alaskan cruise—for the afternoon when Stuart was killed. Oliver had been hanging out with friends but couldn't account for the whole afternoon. Also, if Holly or Oliver had approached the boat in scuba gear, it still didn't explain how or why Liam had been rendered unconscious. Forensic tests done at the time didn't reveal the presence of drugs in the beer or sandwiches, which really didn't prove that he hadn't been dosed. Disposing of tainted food on a boat in the middle of the Pacific wouldn't have been difficult.

"Ava."

She heard his voice in her ear. She sighed and said, "I'm here, Liam." *Here for you.*

"Ava, look out the window." His voice came through the earbud. "I'm using the binoculars, and I see a yellow Jeep Wrangler pulling into the parking lot in front of the cottage."

She bolted to the window in the dining room. She knew only one person who drove a Wrangler. "My brother. Michael."

"Why is he here?"

"I don't know."

She couldn't think of a single reason for him to return to Lincoln County. Too many of the folks in Narcissus had been cruel when he was released from prison. Though he'd been cleared of all charges, they viewed him with suspicion and treated him like a murderer instead of a wrongly accused man.

According to him, the move to Pendleton where he lived in a small cabin and worked at a ranch was to escape memories of his murdered girlfriend and friends who betrayed him. Always a quiet guy, his years in prison made him reclusive...and dark. Some said he'd turned cold, that all his emotions had frozen. Ava didn't believe it. She'd heard him laugh. She'd seen the devilish glint in his eye when he played a practical joke on her. When he got out of the Jeep and slapped his tan cowboy hat on his head, she was happy to see him. Her handsome brother with his sharp blue eyes and sandy hair was one of the people she truly loved.

She dashed for the front door, flung it open and ran to him. He caught both of her hands and whipped her in a wide circle. Instantly, she was transported back in time to when she was ten years old and her older brother took a day off work to be with her. After their father died, Michael Donovan was her chosen male role model.

He set her down on the ground, stepped back, looked into her eyes and frowned. "What's this I hear about you getting hooked up with an accused murderer?"

She gaped. "What?"

"Dammit, Ava. You always did have a thing for bad boys."

Chapter Eight

Listening to the confrontation between Ava and her brother through his earbud, Liam was taken aback. Never before had anyone accused him of being a bad boy. He'd always worked hard and done well in school. He earned a doctorate by the age of twenty-four and was now a tenured professor at U of O. The documentary about his shipwreck recovery expeditions near the Strait of Juan de Fuca compared him to Jacques Cousteau and Indiana Jones. Both were adventurers and educated men, just like him. His cringe turned into a grin. Cousteau and Jones were definitely bad boys. Just. Like. Him.

Sure, he'd picked up a shady reputation for being a treasure hunter—a modern-day pirate. And he'd gone through a phase when he rode a badass Harley, wore leather jackets and drank tequila. He'd been proud of the rep, which probably made him more of a nerd than a real outlaw. Nothing wrong with being a "bad boy."

He heard Ava make a comment to that effect. "You're right, Mikey. I like bad boys. How could I not? Take a look at my brothers."

"Don't put this on me," he said. "You should have learned from the lousy examples set by me and Barry. Be smart, Ava. Don't hook up with a guy who isn't good enough for you."

Silently, Liam agreed. He peered down from the high lighthouse windows at the siblings who faced off in the parking area at the front of the cottage. The brother was a tall, lean cowboy. Ava, dressed in cargo shorts and a white button-down shirt under a khaki anorak, looked like she ought to be on a safari somewhere.

"Oh, yawn," Ava said. "I've heard this lecture before."

"You're right, sis. And I'll say it again. I never liked the condescending way you were treated by Portland Jimmy the lawyer. Then there was that street artist who didn't contribute a nickel toward rent—he was a waste of flesh. Not to mention the guy who claimed to be a descendant from Chief Joseph."

"Stating the obvious, Mikey boy. This is none of your business."

In the nuance of her tone, Liam heard sisterly irritation. His own sister spoke the same way to him. She'd been sympathetic when he was arrested and had set him up with a good lawyer, which was more than his dad had done. An acclaimed virologist, his father was too busy saving the world to worry about his son, who ought to be able to handle something as mundane as a murder allegation by himself. Not that Liam expected his dad to do anything. After Liam's mom died when he was thirteen, Dad pretty much resigned from his parental duties.

"I worry about you," Michael said to his sister.

"Somehow, I doubt that you drove all the way from Pendleton to criticize my former boyfriends."

"Rachel called me," he said. "She's concerned on account of that professor you had a crush on when you were at the university."

"No idea what you're talking about."

"Liam Brody." Her brother's voice rumbled like a volcano about to erupt. "I'm talking about Dr. Liam Brody, the guy in the newspapers who is accused of murder. Rachel said you wanted to date him six years ago when you took his class, but he was too old for you, not to mention he was your teacher."

"What's with you guys?" she grumbled. "All I did was send Rachel a text telling her that I wanted to drop by her potluck this afternoon before I had my regular weekly appointment with Georgina."

"Right," he said, "and she texted back, asking if you'd heard anything about Brody. And you replied 'w/e.' I guess that stands for *whatever.* She knew you were hiding something."

Apparently, Ava resented her sister's conclusion, because she let loose with a fusillade of hostility—none of which included actual profanity—aimed at both brother and sister. Liam stifled an urge to chuckle. He would have given a lot to have his family worry about him as much as her brother and sister obviously cared about her. Though not happy about being characterized as the next loser boyfriend destined to ruin Ava's life, he'd like to meet the rest of the Donovan family in person.

When Ava ran out of words, her brother said, "I'll give you a ride to Rachel's house."

"Another thing," she said, "you and our snarky sis were so busy finding fault with my possible choice of a mate that you missed the headline. You're as blind as a couple of big-eared bats. From what's been reported in the paper and on TV, the case against Liam is totally circumstantial."

"So now it's *Liam*, is it?"

"Missing the point, butthead. He's in the same position you were."

"Not hardly." Liam heard Michael scoff before he continued. "I got scooped up by a couple of cops who weren't gentle about throwing me into custody."

"Jessop?" she asked.

"Matter of fact, Jess-hole was front and center. I still have the scars. After he and his sadistic buddies locked me up and assigned me an inexperienced public defender, I never got out on bail. You know that's how it went, Ava. I was convicted before I appeared in court. The trial was a sham. I never had a chance of beating the charges."

"Oh, Michael." Her voice broke, and Liam heard her sniffle. "I'm so sorry for what happened to you."

"Your professor has a respectable job, important friends and a wealthy family. He's been handled with care, and I'm guessing he has a high-class, expensive lawyer, probably hired a private investigator. Brody was granted bail. He's been spending this time before the trial at his home. So far, he's gotten a damn good deal."

"What if he's found guilty?" she asked in the same shaky voice. "What if he's innocent and goes to jail? Just like you."

"Not doing himself any favors by skipping out on bail."

"Shouldn't he do everything he can to find the truth?"

Liam listened as the silent pause grew longer. Finally, Michael said, "I understand. No innocent man should ever be incarcerated. But I'm warning you, Ava Caitlyn Donovan, don't get involved with this guy. You'll end up being hurt."

Though Liam wanted a chance to rebut Michael, he didn't want to make his plea to Ava through their walkie-talkie device. Her true feelings showed more in her body language, and seeing her physical reactions helped him understand her. Better he should wait until they were alone face-to-face to tell her that he would never intentionally hurt her.

He watched while she and her brother talked about family things, including their mom's current good health, Barry's latest breakup with a girlfriend and Rachel's third-grade daughter winning a spelling bee. Finally, Ava sent her brother on his way with a promise to meet him at Rachel's house. She needed to drive herself because she was going to see

Georgina after. When Michael left, Liam watched his yellow Wrangler drive away on the narrow road leading back to the route through the Siuslaw National Forest. He threw a burner phone, his laptop, water bottle and energy bars into his backpack before descending the knotted rope to the floor.

Though he hadn't noticed watchers in the surrounding forest, Liam took care and dodged behind cover on his way to the barn behind the cottage. Ava had left the side door unlocked, and he darted inside. The old structure, with the high, gambrel roof, a spacious loft and wide double doors, was more ramshackle than the other buildings on the property. Several of the weathered boards had rotted away, leaving gaps. In the early 1900s when the lighthouse was built, the barn must have been used as a stable for horses. Later, it made a convenient storage space for cars, trucks and other equipment.

Parked at the front was a four-door Sonata. Liam spoke into his mic. "I'm in the barn."

"Be right there," she said. "Did you listen to everything my brother said?"

"Being called a 'bad boy' is kind of cool."

"Yeah, neat-o." Her voice oozed with sarcasm. "Mikey also admitted that he understood why you wanted to investigate. You know, it might not be a bad idea if we got—"

"See you in a minute." He purposely interrupted, guessing that she was about to suggest they recruit her family to help investigate. No way. When he wrote his *Fugitive on the Run Handbook*, one of the cardinal rules would be: no family. The last thing he wanted was to get the entire Donovan clan accused of being accessories.

Ava LUGGED AN insulated bag filled with food, juice drinks and water. She also carried a sleeping bag and a tarp to the garage where Liam would hide in the trunk of her Hyundai for their trip to Narcissus. Her sixteen-year-old Toyota Tacoma truck would have provided a more comfortable hiding place if she'd installed the cover over the cargo bed, but she'd been using her truck to transport construction equipment and junk to the dump. Cleaning it up and putting on the cover might look suspicious. She could practically hear Jessop's scratchy voice demanding to know what she was hiding. *Nothing much. Just an escaped fugitive.*

Seeing Michael and hearing him fuss about her former boyfriends made her both happy and sad. Cheerful because she truly loved her family and was glad they cared. Miserable due to the secret she was keeping from them. Liam's presence loomed larger and more dangerous than an elephant in the room. Bigger than a wooly mammoth. How could she keep denying his presence?

At the barn, she pulled open the double doors, went inside and closed the doors again. Liam stepped out of the shadows behind the riding mower. Though his jaw was outlined with stubble and his thick dark hair looked like he'd combed it with a turbo-drill, his easy grin told her that freedom agreed with him.

"Sleep well?" she asked.

"Surprisingly, yes." He stepped up beside her, opened the rear passenger door of the Sonata and started placing her stuff inside. "The rhythm of the surf is a lullaby for me."

"You miss your dive boat."

"Damn right, I do. These weeks while my travel has been restricted feel like years. When this is over, I want to take a long trip, maybe to Cozumel. Ever been there?"

"Never have." But she'd heard about the incredible scuba diving along the Mesoamerican reef system, the languorous heat, white sandy beaches and palm trees. She'd spent very little time in tropical climates—so different from the rugged Oregon coast. Traveling there with Liam, diving with him, sailing with him sounded like a fantasy come true. "Maybe someday."

"Soon."

"You're awfully confident."

"Visualizing a positive outcome keeps me sane."

"Right." She'd never thought of him as the type to make a vision board. Liam seemed more like her, basing his plans on research and knowledge of the past. "Do you believe in happily-ever-after?"

"I need to. Especially now."

Leaving the passenger door open, she took the sleeping bag and circled to the rear and opened the trunk. After she smoothed the tarp and the unzipped bag inside, she unloaded a small stash of food and water bottles. Stepping back, she peered into the small but cozy nest. "Are you going to fit in there?"

"I'll make it work."

She scrutinized him from the top of his six-foot-two-inch height to his broad chest and shoulders to his extra-large boots. "If we clear out the back of the truck and put the cover over the bed, you'd have enough room to stretch out."

"And it's the first place anybody would look."

So true. She tried another suggestion. "If you're too cramped, the seats in the back fold down and make the trunk larger. The latches on each side are broken, so you can reach them from inside the trunk and put the back down."

"Got it," he said as he climbed into the trunk, folded his long body and closed the trunk over his head.

The rear of the Hyundai bounced while Liam shifted his position. Doubtful about the viability of pulling this off, Ava shook her head. This scheme felt unpracticed and haphazard. They'd never get away with it. Speaking in a normal voice which would be picked up by her mic, she said, "We should rethink."

"It'll work. Can you hear me through the earbud?"

"Loud and clear."

The jostling from the trunk stilled. "Ready," he said.

She opened the barn door, drove out and closed it again. In minutes, she was on the two-lane road through the old-growth forest, leaving the coast behind. Last night's rain had renewed the moss-covered trees and undergrowth of ferns. New leaves on hemlock, alder and maple wore a brilliant green. The towering Sitka spruce, some over three hundred years old, reached up and touched the clouds.

Though Ava loved the drama of crashing waves and screaming gulls at seaside, the primordial forests of Oregon gave her a sense of peace and calm. The winds that shrieked on the coast turned to whispers in the forest, offering reassurance that all was for the best. Nature would always take care of itself.

She heard Liam's voice through her earbud. "I've got a couple of things for you to focus on when you talk to your sister. Number one is Oliver Whitcomb, the seventeen-year-old son."

"Holly's son. That makes them Holly and Ollie," she said. "You don't really think he killed his father, do you?"

"It's possible. I've gone diving with the kid a couple of times. He's quiet and smart. I like him, and he doesn't seem like a killer. But I need to consider everybody as a suspect. Oliver might be responsible for drugging me."

"Why?"

"He and his father could have been plotting together. More than once, I've caught Stuart trying to sell artifacts we rescued from shipwrecks. He might have recruited his son to help funnel the artifacts to a fence. All they needed was to get me out of the way."

"Are you saying that you were actually the target of the assault?"

"They didn't want to kill me," Liam said. "Stuart invited me to come onto the yacht. We were a long way offshore when I passed out. There were no other boats in sight. Not sure how long I was unconscious, but it was at least a half hour. Plenty of time to shove me overboard and get me out of the way."

"Which means you weren't meant to be murdered."

"Correct."

She shook her head. His logic didn't add up. "Why would Stuart get his son involved? What did he hope to gain by drugging you?"

"If Ollie planned to kill his dad, I made a convenient fall guy to be blamed for the crime."

Though she'd only met Oliver once or twice, Ava found it hard to believe this young man—a typical teenager—had the smarts or the devious intentions of a criminal mastermind. "Why would he want to hurt his father? How is this related to missing artifacts? Or to drugs?"

"Not an airtight theory."

"More holes than a colander," she said. "Why do you think Rachel might know about Oliver Whitcomb? Her oldest kid is in third grade."

"Your sister works in a pharmacy," he said. "She hears a lot of gossip and might have information about drugs."

"She's an assistant, not a pharmacist. And I seriously doubt she'd have better, more accurate information than the forensic people who tested the food and drink on the yacht and did a tox screen on you."

Ava drove along the coast on Highway 101 for a few miles before turning onto the river road that led to her hometown.

She'd reviewed the information Liam collected and hoped he'd come up with better theories than blaming Oliver. "What else should I ask Rachel about?"

"I'm looking for motivations that wouldn't be included in police data. Was Holly dating? Maybe she has a jealous boyfriend. What about other people who hated Stuart? Who benefits financially if he's out of the way? What about his sister, Serena?"

"I doubt she'll be at a potluck hosted by Rachel. Not high-class enough for her."

"But she dated your brother Barry."

"Occasionally, she goes slumming with the likes of the Donovans."

She heard him chuckle. "According to Stuart's will, Ollie inherits his shares in Deep Dive, and Holly is the executrix which puts her in charge."

"I saw that in your research. You still maintain the majority share of the stock, but if you sell, you need to pay her off for the sale of the boats and equipment. That could add up to serious money."

"That's the kind of gossip I want to hear," he said. "I'm guessing that Stuart is one of the very few murder victims from Narcissus. People have got to be talking about him. Were there special reasons that Holly and Ollie or anybody else wanted Stuart dead?"

Entering the city limits of Narcissus, she slowed to twenty-five miles per hour. The last thing she wanted was to be cited for speeding by Jess-hole or any of the other local cops. This former lumber town had definitely seen better days. Several shops on Main were boarded over with graffiti-marked par-ticleboard. An Open sign hung in the door of the bakery, and the twinkle lights outlining Fresh Daily were lit. Through the windows of the corner diner, she saw a couple of guys in flannel shirts who could have been great-grandsons of original Narcissus residents. The pharmacy where Rachel worked was closed on Sunday as was a tiny bookstore and an antique shop. Mack's Lumberjack Tavern with blinking neon signs in every window had several cars parked in the slanted parking spaces.

When she stopped at the one and only stoplight in town, she looked over and saw three men standing on the sidewalk outside the tavern and smoking. One of them leaned down and stared into her Sonata. Her gaze met his, and she gasped. "Tancredo," she said. "I think he recognizes me."

He signaled for her to pull over. "He wants me to park. Should I see what he wants?"

"Not now," Liam said. "Give him a smile and a wave. Then drive on."

"Agreed." It was like he'd read her mind. She didn't want to get entangled with this guy. Feigning confusion, she waved and tapped the accelerator. The light hadn't changed.

Moving with a speed and agility she didn't expect from a gray-haired, wizened man, Tancredo crossed the sidewalk, hopped off the curb and grabbed the door handle on the passenger side. The door was locked. He yanked on the handle. With his other hand, he slapped the glass.

"Pull over, Ava Donovan," his gravelly voice commanded. "I want to talk to you."

His palm flattened on the window. He was missing his fourth finger and pinkie.

Chapter Nine

Ava had no choice. If she followed her instincts and drove away at top speed, she'd hurt Tancredo's good hand and make an enemy for life. She shouted, "Let go of the door. I'll pull over to the curb."

When he stepped back, she rounded the corner and parked at the curb. In her ear, Liam spoke in a quiet but tense voice. "Get away from him as soon as you can. He's dangerous, possibly involved in illegal drug smuggling."

Though she didn't know Tancredo very well, she'd never liked the guy. He exuded the sneering superiority of a boss who—for some unknown reason—considered himself to be better than everybody else. From Liam's research, she recalled the suspicion of illegal drugs. In a way, smuggling made sense for Tancredo. As the harbormaster of a mid-size port, he had the necessary access for shifting goods and cargo from one ship to another. He'd been considered a suspect for Stuart's murder and investigated by the police. According to Liam's notes, he had a solid, believable alibi.

As soon as she parked, he rapped on the window. "Unlock the door."

Again, there was no way to avoid his request without appearing suspicious. When he opened the door of the Sonata and slipped inside, he brought a stench with him. The stink

of sweat that stained his long-sleeved cotton shirt mingled
with the odors of dead and decaying fish, oil and garbage.
His long gray hair crawled out from a filthy baseball cap and
hung in greasy tangles around his grizzled cheeks.

Ava just couldn't force herself to smile. "I haven't seen
you in a long time."

"Hardly recognized you with the short hair." He wheezed
and coughed. "Glad I did. I've got a question for you."

When he closed the door, shutting himself in beside her,
she felt trapped. "If you don't mind, make it quick. I'm in
kind of a hurry."

"Rushing to meet with Georgina, eh? Never thought I'd
see the day when the high-and-mighty Solomon family lowered themselves to talk to a Donovan girl."

"Surprise, surprise." How did he know so much? The
rumor mill in Narcissus and nearby Newport must be operating at full tilt if the men who spent their weekend at the
Lumberjack's Tavern were talking about her and Georgina.

Speaking through the earbud, Liam whispered, "Ask him
about the quarter-of-a-million-dollar loan he made to Stuart."

She turned her head to scrutinize the old man who didn't
look like he had two nickels to rub together. "The Solomons
aren't the only ones with money. I heard that you made a very
large cash loan to Stuart."

He squinted at her. "Now, where would you hear something like that? One of your bigmouth brothers?"

"Is it true? A quarter of a million? I thought Stuart's family was rich."

"He and Serena squandered their inheritances." His lower
lip stuck out in a frown. "Stuart bought that fancy cabin
cruiser—the boat where he died—before he got around to
paying me back."

"Why did you make the loan?"

"He was supposed to do a job for me."

A job? That could be anything. She tried to pry deeper without seeming too interested. "Did you get your money's worth?"

"Maybe. Maybe not." His voice turned hostile, almost threatening. "What's it to you?"

"Just curious." She backed off, not wanting to anger him. "I like to know things."

"You were always the smart one in your family," he said. "Little Ava went to college and met a professor. Liam Brody. I heard he's in touch with you."

Who would tell him that? "Let me guess. You've been talking to Deputy Jessop."

"I knew you were smart." He wheezed again, and she realized that the noise represented laughter. "I need to get a message to Brody."

Inadvertently, she glanced toward the back seat. If Tancredo knew Liam was so close, he'd tear out the seat cushions to get at him. "What's the message?"

"Strictly business, little girl." He stared through the windshield at the quiet streets of Narcissus on a Sunday. "His dive boat is moored at Newport. It's an older craft but well maintained. I've been aboard a couple of times."

"No," Liam said through the earbud. "He's never been aboard with me."

"Have you, indeed," Ava asked being careful not to accuse him of lying.

"With Stuart Whitcomb," Tancredo said. "I can vouch for the seaworthiness of the boat, and I've had a couple of offers from people who are interested."

"Why do they think Dr. Brody's boat is for sale?"

"Bargain hunters." He gave another grotesque laugh. "Some people think he might need quick money for his legal defense. They expect your favorite professor is going to jail."

"What do you think?"

"I don't care if he's guilty or not. Not my problem. All I want is to get some of my money back. Tell Brody I'll handle the sale for a 25 percent commission."

"That's a little steep."

"Yeah, and he's in no position to complain."

Liam spoke quietly through the earbud. "Ask for names. Who wants to buy my fleet?"

Though she wanted this conversation to be over, her voice stayed calm and steady. "If I should happen to see or hear from Professor Brody, who should I tell him is interested in purchasing his property?"

"Peter Quincy mentioned the possibility. And Serena Whitcomb." He downed the window of the Sonata, stuck out his head and spat on the sidewalk. "I'd demand cash or a cashier's check from that bitch. I don't trust her."

"What's your problem with Serena?"

"I hate the damn Whitcomb family," he said, dragging his shirtsleeve across his mouth and inadvertently giving her a close-up view of his three-fingered left hand. The remaining digits and thumb were filthy. Grime crusted beneath the nails. "Their grandpappy cheated mine and drove him out of business. The Tancredo family—my folks—should have been rich lumber barons. Instead, I had to get a job at the mill. I should have owned that damn place. It's where I lost my fingers."

"I didn't know your family had such deep roots."

"My grandpappy sank into a funk after he lost the business. Died young. Some say he killed himself. The rest of my kin scattered and moved on. I blame anybody named Whitcomb."

This old grudge sounded like a motive to her. "You must have been pleased when Stuart was murdered."

"You can tell Brody thanks from me." He flung open the car door. "Don't be a stranger, Ava Donovan."

As she returned to the route leading to Rachel's house, she put down the windows and allowed the breeze to blow away the smell of Tancredo. A bitter man. A hostile man. But was he a murderer? "Seems like Tancredo would want to keep Stuart alive so he could get his investment repaid."

"He's a tough nut to crack," Liam said. "Why was he on my dive boat?"

"Your partner must have invited him."

"If he hates the Whitcomb family as much as he says, why make a loan to Stuart? Why talk to Serena about selling my dive boat?"

"It's about power," she said. "I can imagine a scum bucket like Tancredo lording it over Stuart and demanding his money. The same for Serena."

"That fits," he said. "I've been doing business with Tancredo for years, and he loves to give citations for breaking rules. This is the first I've heard about his grandfather and the feud with Stuart's family. I probably should have paid more attention to the old guy."

"Same here."

At the outer edge of town, Ava drove past the three huge buildings for processing raw lumber. Two had closed down. One remained open and manufactured particleboard. The chemical stench of the process hung in the air. Her father used to talk about his days at the mill when he made a decent salary and could support his wife and five children. He died not long after he was laid off from that job. Long ago, Narcissus thrived. Not anymore.

"Almost there," she announced to Liam as she turned onto a smaller two-lane road. "How are you doing back there?"

"I'm okay. Eating your excellent macadamia cookies."

She took a left and then turned right and then to the end of a block lined with one- and two-story rectangular houses in various colors of wood siding popular in the post–World War II era. The unimaginative architecture was saved from being boring by flourishing trees and gardens. Double rows of daffodils and narcissus, namesake of the town, marched across the front yard of Rachel's two-story, sky-blue house.

A couple dozen people milled in the front yard, including Michael, Barry and her other brother, Jerome. Rachel's grade school kids chased three other boys who were slightly older. Ava recognized several other people who were standing around and chatting.

"Fish Finley is here," she reported to Liam.

"I'd like to hear what he's going to say as a witness."

The crowd parted, and she saw her sister talking to a tall, slender woman with wavy, blond hair tumbling to her shoulders. She wore purple and yellow activewear topped by a matching jacket. "Holly Louise Whitcomb. She's here."

Ava checked her reflection in the visor mirror and fluffed her bangs. She'd be able to ask direct questions and get answers straight from the horse's mouth.

HIDING INSIDE THE too-small trunk, Liam listened to a cacophony of voices, punctuated by the laughter of children and the sound of the Hyundai's back door being opened and closed. The Sunday gathering of the Donovan clan and their friends exploded like the launch of a space rocket. He heard Ava ask, "What are you all doing out here in the front yard?"

"Waiting for you," said a man whose voice he recognized as Michael. "About time."

"We're getting ready to play touch football," a youthful male explained. "The front yard is bigger than the back and has the sidewalk running down the middle to separate the sides."

Michael added, "Rachel won't let us play in the back because we'll mess up the tables with the potluck."

"That's right," said an authoritative woman, probably Rachel herself. "We'll leave you footballers to it. Anybody who would rather eat and be civilized, come with me."

"I brought cookies," Ava said.

"And I appreciate your effort," Rachel said. "Listen, I'm sorry Michael is being a jerk. I didn't tell him to bother you at the lighthouse."

"It's okay. Gave me a chance to explain my opinion on Dr. Brody."

"Which is?"

"Innocent until proven guilty," she said firmly. "I don't think he killed Stuart, and there isn't substantial evidence to convict him."

"Come on, Ava. I know you used to like this guy, but he's guilty, guilty, guilty. He and Stuart went out to sea, then Stuart got clobbered and died. Did I mention that nobody else was on the boat?"

"Dr. Brody was unconscious." Ava piped up to defend him, and Liam was proud of her. He didn't seem to have much other support. She continued, "While Liam was out cold, the murderer could have sailed up and boarded or gotten close on a scuba dive."

"Oh, sure. Maybe the killer rode a dolphin. Or an orca."

"When Dr. Brody woke, he tried to revive Stuart, and he called the Coast Guard. If he killed Stuart, why not just dump the body overboard and sail back to the marina?"

"Who can understand the mind of a murderer?"

Another female voice chimed in. "Ava makes a good point.

If Brody meant to kill Stuart, he could have easily gotten away with it. No need to call the authorities."

"Good to see you, Holly Louise," Ava said. "I'm sorry for your loss."

Liam concentrated hard, trying to catch a hint of Holly's emotional state in the tone of her voice. Was she in mourning for Stuart? They'd been married for nearly sixteen years and were parents to a son. Would she miss her ex-husband? Liam knew for a fact that Stuart hadn't been faithful or thoughtful. For a long time, he and Liam had shared a part-time assistant. A salty old widow named Maxine, she was the only person who remembered anniversaries and birthdays for Stuart. What was her last name? Gallo, Maxine Gallo. She'd bought the presents, sent the cards and the occasional bouquets of red roses when Stuart took off for a weekend without his wife on board.

Had Maxine Gallo been contacted by Liam's overpriced attorney? She knew both owners of Deep Dive better than they knew each other, which wasn't to say much. Liam and Stuart hadn't been the sort of friends who shared intimate secrets. The first he'd heard of Stuart's divorce was *after* he'd served Holly with papers. She must have been angry with him. Did she hate him? Want him dead?

"I always liked Liam," Holly said. "He was a real gentleman. Good sense of humor. And not bad to look at."

"I've heard that before," Rachel said. "From Ava."

"Of course, I liked him. He was a terrific professor."

"And not bad to look at," Rachel teased. "Am I right?"

He heard Ava clear her throat before she jumped in with both feet instead of politely tiptoeing around the edge of the topic. "What do you think, Holly? Did Liam kill Stuart?"

"Of course not," Holly said.

"Who did?"

For a moment, Ava's blunt question put an end to their chat. In the trunk, Liam listened with bated breath. He hoped the uncomfortable silence wouldn't last too long.

"Off the top of my head," Holly said, "I can think of a dozen people who wanted my ex-husband dead. People he insulted or cheated or lied to. They've talked to me because, obviously, I'm not the head cheerleader of the Stuart Whitcomb Fan Club. Let's start with Charlie Tancredo. My dear ex-husband borrowed a bunch of money from him, off the books."

"Wait," Ava said. "Why would Tancredo kill him before he got paid back?"

"Stuart made it clear that he wasn't going to pay. After he died, Charlie came to me, and I promised to work something out when I've gotten my payoff. I feel bad about my son racing around in a fancy cabin cruiser bought with Tancredo's money."

Ava spoke up. "That's very fair-minded of you."

"And I don't want Tancredo as an enemy," Holly said. "If you're looking for motives, you might as well count me. Oliver will inherit the stock and I'll be his executrix because my dumb ex-husband never changed his will."

"Who else?" Ava asked.

Holly rattled off several names. "My ex wasn't a likable guy. He always wanted everything to be in perfect order. Actually, he demanded it. My therapist said he had OCD—obsessive-compulsive disorder—and I think she was right."

Liam had to agree. Stuart was a stickler for details—a trait he called "perfectionism." OCD was far more accurate. He actually enjoyed the detailed paperwork required to keep track of their inventory. Liam often found him humming while he hunched over a notebook or ledger.

Holly continued, "Then there are all the husbands and

boyfriends of women he dated. Long list. A couple of them showed up at the house and popped him in the nose. The police have records because, of course, Stuart insisted on filing charges."

"Wow," Ava said. "I had no idea. Was there anybody else? Anybody who stands out?"

"The husband of your benefactor. Peter Quincy."

"Really? I know he runs a competing salvage business, but I never thought exploring shipwrecks was a cutthroat business."

"Quincy and Stuart were a couple of pirates. Draw your own conclusions."

Liam wished they had been questioning Holly under oath and could compel her to explain everything she knew about the connection between those two swashbucklers. Quincy was suspected of working with Tancredo and drug smuggling for northern cartels. Could he also be fencing artifacts from Deep Dive salvage operations?

The rest of the conversation with Stuart's ex-wife turned to local gossip and congratulations on Rachel's third-grade daughter's win in the spelling bee. After Holly moved away, Rachel did a "tsk-tsk-tsk."

"What?" Ava asked.

"Poor Holly! She's still hung up on that slimebag ex-husband. Did you notice? She still wears her wedding-engagement ring set. Platinum and diamond."

"I noticed. Big sparklers. It's got to be worth a lot."

"Over twenty-five thousand," Rachel said. "That's what Holly told me."

"Doesn't really go with the workout clothes."

"Uh-oh." Rachel swore under her breath. Still loud enough for Liam to hear. "Here comes trouble."

"Serena Whitcomb," Ava said for Liam's benefit. "What's she doing here? Rachel, did you invite her?"

"Do you think I've lost my mind? Come with me, sis. You and I have to stop her before she crashes headlong into Holly."

That face-off sounded like a potential disaster to Liam. He doubted anything good would come from these two women meeting. Selfishly, he thought their conflict might put a new perspective on the murder.

Chapter Ten

Ava managed to drop off her platter of macadamia nut cookies on one of the picnic tables on the patio before she fell into step with her sister. Together, they marched across the backyard to protect Holly from Serena Whitcomb. As they approached the shady maple in the corner of Rachel's neatly landscaped property, all three Donovan brothers stepped up to flank them, standing in support of Holly Louise.

Rachel spoke first. "I'm surprised to see you, Serena. Our little neighborhood potluck doesn't seem like your kind of party."

"You have an awfully short memory." Though she was average height, Serena looked down her nose at all of them. With her black hair styled in graceful tresses, her complexion perfectly tanned and her fingernails professionally manicured, she was polished and impressive. "When I dated Barry, I was here every week. I even gave you my housekeeper's recipe for enchiladas."

Sheepishly, Barry said, "Sorry to hear about Stuart. We all came to the memorial service, you know. How are you holding up?"

"I'm all right." Ava glimpsed a flicker of sadness in Serena's expression before she pinched her lips together and glared at them with her dark brown eyes. "If you really cared about my brother, you'd never invite his bitter ex-wife to your gathering."

"Not so bitter," Holly snapped. "I'm going to inherit more than you."

Rachel wrapped her arms around Holly—half to protect her and half to hold her back. "She's been my best friend since fifth grade."

"What about me?" Serena stamped her little foot in her Gucci designer sandals. Her toenails were the same bright red as her fingernails. "I've lived here for three generations."

"But you went to some fancy-pants prep school in New York. We never bonded. And you're at least five years older than I am."

Ava could see tempers rising. Hoping to cool the situation, she stepped between the two feuding women. "Why don't you come with me, Serena? We can get a plate of food and some iced tea."

"Don't try to push me around, Ava. There are a few things I need to say to Holly, and the brat won't return my phone calls."

Holly came at her. "I don't want to talk to you."

"Fine. We'll meet in court." Serena flipped open her red Birkin bag and reached inside. "I've got the paperwork right here."

Standing beside Serena, Ava was the only one who could see inside the purse that had probably cost more than her Sonata. She saw the small gun, probably a .45 like hers but metallic. The weapon looked far more lethal than her bubble gum pink Glock.

Before Ava could say anything, Serena snapped her purse closed before handing off the paperwork. Her eyes narrowed to laser-focused slits. Barry stepped up beside her and took her arm. With a pivot, he spun her away from the others and aimed her toward the buffet table. "Let me get you something to drink. You must be thirsty."

Because threating people was dehydrating? Serena's response to her ex-boyfriend went from outrage to seductive as she placed her long, slim fingers on his hand. "I'd like a martini."

"I'm sure you would."

While Barry escorted her away, Ava watched with concern. The gun in the Birkin worried her.

"Mission accomplished," Michael said. "That's why nobody messes with the Donovan family or their friends. Holly, where's your son?"

"Out front, playing football with the rest of the teenagers. At least, I hope he's playing. Oliver has been depressed since his father's murder."

Michael took charge of Holly. "Do you want to talk about him?"

She nodded. "It's been hard for him to lose his dad."

Ava's youngest brother, Jerome, glanced between his two sisters. "Are you guys okay?"

Ava wondered if she ought to mention the gun. She knew other people who carried weapons but not to a potluck on a Sunday afternoon. What did Serena have in mind? Surely, she wouldn't open fire here. She wasn't homicidal. Was she?

She nodded to Jerome. "See you tomorrow at the lighthouse."

"Cool. We need to go over specs on the plumbing. How many new bathrooms in the cottage and where should we put them?"

"I'll have answers for you tomorrow."

While she strolled back toward the patio, Ava heard Liam's voice in her ear. He had a ton of questions, but she couldn't begin to answer his concerns until they could talk face-to-face. She allowed Rachel to direct her toward the array of potluck dishes. Ice-filled coolers held soft drinks and beer.

"On the kitchen counter where the kids can't reach," Rachel said, "I have Pinot Noir, Zinfandel and Chardonnay from our fine local wineries."

"I'm not drinking," Ava said. "As soon as I leave, I have to check in with my—what did Holly call her?—my benefactor, Georgina."

"I don't envy you that meeting. I mean, your work at the lighthouse is very cool, but Georgina and her snooty family creep me out almost as much as Serena and the other Whitcombs."

"After I complete the renovation, Georgina is going to be looking for someone to manage her bed-and-breakfast. You'd be a natural for the job."

"So true," Rachel said, not bragging but stating a fact. "I bake, I clean and I have impeccable taste. But I already have a job."

"Do you ever think about going back to school to become a pharmacist? Sooner or later, your boss is going to retire and you could take over."

"Thanks for your opinion, pushy pants. Just because you're my sis, you don't get to call the shots for me. Unless you want me bugging you about settling down and having babies."

"You like working in the pharmacy, don't you?" Ava hoped to ease into the topic of drugs. Her sister was sharp and intuitive. Rachel would recognize a direct inquiry for what it was—an attempted interrogation. "And you already know so much about various prescriptions and their side effects."

"Sorting and preparing the dosage is similar to following a recipe for baking," Rachel said. "But I wouldn't like the responsibility of monitoring somebody else's medicine."

"Especially now, when so many people are addicted."

"That's the truth. Even here in our puny, little town." Rachel exhaled a sigh. "I spend half my time verifying prescriptions from doctors in Portland and Salem. A lot of people have to be cut off."

"Anybody we know?"

"Ava Caitlyn Donovan! I can't believe you asked me that. I'm a professional. I respect boundaries."

"Sorry. Just curious."

"Between you and me, addicts don't come to the pharmacy to get their fix. Good, old Charlie Tancredo is apparently dumb enough to loan money to Stuart. Also, Tancredo is a prescription drug pusher."

Good to know. It was another loose end for Liam to report to his attorney.

INSIDE THE TRUNK, Liam shifted positions, flexed his shoulders and back. Ava's conversations with various locals didn't interest him until she approached Fish Finley, who had been working regularly at the lighthouse as a subcontractor. Liam conjured a mental image of Fish with puckered lips like a parrotfish, a slender frame and a shaved head. Fish was a disappointment to him. Liam thought they had a decent relationship, but Fish signed up on the prosecution's side to testify about an argument he'd overheard between Liam and Stuart.

In his quiet voice, Fish introduced Ava to his fiancee. "Her name is Bonnie, and we're getting married. Show her the ring, honey."

"Congratulations," Ava said. "Have you set the date?"

"Better be soon," Bonnie said with a giggle. "Otherwise, I'm going to start showing. I'm four months pregnant."

"Double congratulations. You both look very happy."

"That we are," Fish said. "Hey, I didn't know you and Liam were friends."

"I took a class from him in college. We're not that close."

Not that close? Liam dismissed his irritation at her brush-off comment. She couldn't tell anyone about their relationship, not until they concluded their investigation. The cramped space in the trunk had begun to heat up and tighten around him. The air felt stuffy. He wished he could climb out and walk around, head up his own investigation.

"I helped with some of those classes," Fish said. "I always liked being with Liam on the boat. He never talked down to me, never treated me like I wasn't good enough."

"You are good enough," his girlfriend said. "You're the best."

Once again, Ava was blunt. "I heard you were going to testify at the trial. Is that true?"

"Wish I'd never made that agreement. Don't seem right."

"Why is that?"

"I don't think Liam is a killer, but I know what I heard. I've just got to tell the truth."

"You'd better be sure about what you overheard." Ava's tone sharpened. "Otherwise, it's perjury."

"No way," Bonnie said. "My man always does the right thing."

Liam wasn't so certain. He bent his elbow and tried to reach the back of his neck where sweat prickled. Tomorrow when Fish showed up for work at the lighthouse, he'd have another chance to dig out the truth.

After Fish and Bonnie made their excuses, Ava whispered into her mic. "Not sure if you can hear me, but it's my impression that Fish is lying about what he heard. Or putting a weird slant on it. Something strange is going on with him."

"I think you're right. How soon can we leave?"

"Getting uncomfortable?"

"How soon?"

"I'll go right now. Sit tight."

As if he had a choice? Liam twisted onto his side and silently reviewed the new information they'd learned. Holly had spouted half a dozen names of jilted boyfriends and spouses who had reason to hate Stuart, but Liam doubted any of them had committed this complicated murder that required drugging him, boarding the boat and assaulting Stuart without having him fight back. Both Tancredo and Holly had also mentioned the quarter-of-a-million-dollar loan to Stuart who was expected to perform some kind of service. And there was Rachel's not-too-subtle accusation about the harbormaster of the Newport docks pushing illegal prescription meds. Though Liam's attorney had deposed Tancredo, he hadn't been considered a suspect because his alibi was good.

Making progress. Liam's instinct to pursue his own investigation had been validated. Now he needed to get a message to his legal team: interview Tancredo in depth, check his finances and his access to prescription drugs. Holly had reminded him of the former assistant for Deep Dive who knew many of Stuart's secrets. Maxine Gallo needed to be interviewed.

And Liam would talk to Fish Finley. It was no big surprise that he'd heard Stuart and Liam arguing. Like many partners, they had disagreements that had never turned violent. What was Fish going to tell the prosecutor? Was he lying?

So much to do and so little time to do it. Liam squeezed his eyelids closed and shut down his brain. He couldn't think anymore. His limbs cramped tight. Though he didn't feel particularly heated, his entire body was sweating. This must be what suffocation felt like.

His consciousness shifted, and he inadvertently slipped

into the meditative state where his memories came clearer. He imagined hearing the sounds of gulls and the lapping of waves against the hull of the cabin cruiser. His last memory had been the putt-putt of an outboard motor approaching. In his mind, he was aboard the boat right before Stuart was killed.

The vision of that day was sharp but disjointed, like seeing reflections in a broken mirror. A piece of sky mingled with the deep gray of the Pacific. Liam caught a glimpse of Stuart. His face twisted in anger. His voice grated as he argued with another man. Another voice. Liam couldn't tell if it was his own voice. Or someone else.

What were they saying? Something about how Stuart had to return what he'd taken. Accusing him of being a scavenger without honor.

Liam jolted back to reality, heard the door to the Hyundai open and close.

"It's me," Ava announced.

His vision of the death scene dissipated and vanished. So close, he was so close to remembering exactly what had happened before he passed out. He felt the car dip as she got behind the steering wheel and started the engine.

"Turn on the air conditioner," he growled. His throat was sore. His voice, hoarse. "Now. Full blast."

"Cranky," she said. "I've never actually locked myself in the trunk, but I'm guessing it gets stifling and hot. Does it smell like oil or more like a spare tire?"

"Air conditioner," he repeated.

When he felt the car lurch forward and zip quietly through the streets of Narcissus, he released the latch that held one of the rear seats in place and collapsed it forward. He stuck his head through the opening and sucked down a gulp of air.

"Sorry I didn't get a chance to talk to Ollie," she chirped.

"He was standing in the front yard, watching the sloppiest football game I've ever seen. The kid looked depressed."

"It's okay. You did a great job getting people to open up."

"We have a problem, and I'm not sure what to do about it." She glanced over her shoulder into the back seat. "I saw something. A gun."

"Where?" He crawled halfway into the back seat but stayed low so he couldn't be seen through the windows. "Who had the gun?"

"Serena. She was carrying it in her purse. A small, gray metal pistol."

The idea of suspects running around with weapons bothered him, but there wasn't much he could do about it. If Deputy Jessop hadn't been such a jerk, Ava could have gone to him for advice. "What about Marshal Woodburn?" he suggested. "He made a big deal of checking your Glock. Maybe if you told him, he could pay Serena a visit."

"I guess I could call him," she said. "Or I could talk to Barry. He used to date Serena, might have even been the one who helped her purchase a weapon. You know, for protection."

In the back seat, Liam reached into the insulated bag she'd packed and took out a water bottle. He unscrewed the top and chugged half. "Can't stay in the trunk. Take me somewhere near Georgina's house and drop me off. I'll get close enough to listen."

"What if you can't hear me?"

"I trust you to ask the right questions," he said. "You're good at this."

"When I was working as a teaching assistant at the university, I figured out how to ask questions and probe for answers. I learned pretty quickly how to identify which answers were lies or a cover-up."

"Which was how you figured out Fish was hiding something."

"His comments about truth-telling sounded a lot like 'the dog ate my homework,'" she said. "I wonder why he'd volunteer to give phony testimony."

The most obvious motive would be a payoff. Somebody could be bribing Fish to lie about an argument he overheard. If he could learn the identity of the payer, they might be on their way to unraveling the murder.

He unfastened the latch on the other back seat, pushed it out of the way and rolled into the rear of the car. *Sweet relief.* Not a lot of space, but the back seat of the Hyundai was luxurious when compared to the trunk. Lying with his back on the folded-down seats, he stretched out his legs. "There's a lot of forest around here. I can find someplace to stay hidden."

"I'm sure you can. When I was a kid, Rachel and I used to sneak around and spy on these crusty people when they had fancy parties."

"Crusty?"

"As in *upper crust.*"

He imagined Ava and her sister creeping through the verdant underbrush like a couple of wide-eyed woodland imps watching the crusty people who probably resembled his wealthy, intellectual, aloof family. His Los Angeles–based sister represented the socialite branch for the Brody brood, and she worked tirelessly on volunteer projects funding the medical research their father pursued. Liam avoided the events she planned and the blind dates she arranged for him. He identified more with the hardworking, energetic Donovan family, who genuinely cared for each other.

"I have a question," Ava said. "How should I get Georgina and her husband to talk about the murder?"

"You didn't have a problem at your sister's house."

"That's different. I don't want to be too blunt with the woman who is signing my paycheck."

He understood what she was saying. She didn't want to blurt out questions that would offend or would cause Georgina to view her with suspicion. "Keep the focus on her. Everybody likes to talk about themselves."

She nodded. "What else?"

"Use your position as an archeologist and historian," he advised. "Tell her you're looking for more information about the history of the area and the lighthouse."

"Actually, I would like more personal stories that I could put together into a book for the tourists who come to stay at Georgina's B and B."

"You took my nautical archeology class," he reminded her, "and we studied shipwrecks, including the *New Carissa*. Georgina's husband runs his salvage business from Newport, and you can talk to him about the famously dangerous coastline."

"Got it."

When Ava guided the Sonata off the two-lane road at the edge of town, he sat up and peered out the window. The old growth forest surrounding the Solomon family's compound formed a towering wall of trees with moss-covered branches and trunks. He glimpsed a nearby creek, shimmering in the sunlight. Blue jays, magpies and crows swooped through the trees, no doubt waiting to scavenge the leftovers from the four nearby mansions.

Ava parked beside a fat, horizontal log bordering a turnaround. "You can see Georgina's house from the top of that hill. I'll be back here to pick you up in about an hour."

"I'll be waiting."

Glad to be free of the suffocating trunk, he opened the door and stepped into the cool, idyllic forest, hoping she'd find significant information for their investigation and happy that they would have more time together later.

Chapter Eleven

Unsettled by the problematic issues she'd uncovered, Ava tried to focus on the details she needed for this meeting. Afterward, she could call Marshal Woodburn and warn him about Serena's gun. And she could talk to Liam about Tancredo, his loan to Stuart and the job he needed done. Then, there was Fish to consider.

Right now, she had to talk to Georgina. First, she'd share an update on the current progress. Then, she'd ask pertinent questions, using the blueprints of the cottage, about the plumbing issues. How many new bathrooms and where should they be placed? Finally, Ava would offer her opinion on integrating lighthouse history into the bed-and-breakfast setting, including a possible tourist book or booklet. She also had paperwork on the project budget and expected completion dates. Most of all, she reminded herself as she walked up the sidewalk to the front door, Ava wouldn't lose sight of her real reason for being here which was, of course, the investigation.

Georgina might be able to shed light on the motives for Stuart's murder. She and Ava didn't always agree, but Ava had come to respect the other woman's sharp critical eye and most of her opinions about style and taste. Mrs. Solomon Quincy knew a whole different set of Narcissus residents.

As she pressed the doorbell, Ava whispered into her mic, "Can you hear me?"

"Loud and clear," Liam replied. "I'm not as close as I'd like. Surveillance cameras are all over the place."

"Be careful," she said under her breath.

The heavy oak door swung wide, and Georgina, looking expensively groomed as usual, welcomed her into the largest of the four Solomon houses, built in a sort of cul-de-sac with acres of wooded privacy between them. The exterior of Georgina's three-story house—once owned by the lumber baron patriarch, George Solomon, himself—featured a natural stone tower beside the impressively carved, double-door entryway. A huge sunporch occupied the other side of the entrance. Clear fir tongue-in-groove siding, which was stained light gray, covered most of the house. The architectural design featured dozens of windows, many with leaded glass, and window frames painted hunter green. All topped off by a slate roof.

The interior showed opulent craftsmanship with polished paneling, wainscoting and arched ceilings—some painted and others supported with beams. Many of the built-in shelves, fireplace mantels, staircases, pillars and doors showed off woodworking skill and hand-carvings similar to those at the lightkeeper's cottage. Rustic and yet sophisticated at the same time, most of the carving was done by one artist during the 1920s and '30s. Ava thought he deserved a plaque commemorating his contribution to this northwestern mansion.

Though she appreciated the overall effect of elaborate styling from the plaster cupids of the early 1900s to the sleek 1930s Art Deco, to the mid-century modern, she had a hard time convincing Georgina that the lightkeeper's cottage shouldn't be as ornate. After all, this house belonged to an extremely wealthy man while the cottage was meant to be a dwelling for a commonplace worker and his family.

At a table in a library/office that opened onto the sun deck, Ava spread color samples in shades of white. "I'm trying to match the color that was first used in the entrance and dining room in the 1890s. We don't have color photographs to go by, and the description just says it's white."

Georgina balanced a pair of gold frame readers on the tip of her nose and pursed her lips as she considered the variety. "Some are cool, almost bluish. Others are pale yellow."

"These are all from the Benjamin Moore Historical Collection line. It's impossible to be totally accurate because these walls have been painted over several times. For the sake of consistency, I think we should stick to a palette."

"Orange," Georgina said. The color mimicked the thick, curly hair piled on top of her head in a purposely messy bun with tendrils falling around her cheeks. Casual but stylish in an upper-crust way, she wore a flowing, ombré mauve, silk blouse over snug white capris that showed off her slender legs and the glow that came from a tanning booth rather than exposure to the sun. No tan lines on this lady. No freckles, either. Her full lips spread in a feline grin. "Definitely orange and green."

"A perfect combo to complement mid-century modern designs," Ava said, "but maybe not right for the lightkeeper's cottage. I used to hate my parents' green shag carpet."

"Do you think the palette should be more muted?" Georgina twisted her gold cuff bracelet. "So boring, Ava."

"And not necessarily historically accurate. Some rooms during the late 1800s when the lightkeeper's cottage was built were dark purple or bright gold."

"So, I'm on the right track with orange."

Ava shrugged. "Several descriptions of the colors mention a cozy, rosy atmosphere inside the cottage. One writer talks about bringing the sunshine indoors. The palette, I think, should lean toward warmer colors like red and yellow."

"Which make orange."

"That's a lovely bracelet," Ava said. She'd seen 1920s illustrations of similar designs with rows of tiny gold pyramids alternating with rows of roses. "Do you mind if I ask where you got it?"

"A gift from my hubby. He tried to tell me it was antique, but I'm guessing he picked it up in a secondhand store. Peter is awfully practical and very cheap."

"Mind if I take a photo?" Ava could show it to Liam, and he could verify if the bracelet was actually antique and had come from a salvage operation. *Possibly illustrating a connection between Peter Quincy and Stuart.* She snapped the picture using her phone.

Georgina pointed to a creamy white sample. "That one."

"Good pick." They wouldn't get started with the painting until they were approaching the last phase of renovation. "We need to prepare these colors and wallpaper samples for the National Historical Society before actually making the changes and purchasing furniture."

"Shopping," Georgina said with obvious relish. "I can't wait to get started on that part of the process."

"We can do a lot of that online and by visiting specialized furniture stores and shops that can repair the pieces worth saving."

"In terms of the cottage, what are you working on right now?"

Solving the crime of the century? Instead of being blunt, Ava introduced the topic Liam had suggested. "Plumbing. We need to go over the blueprints so you can indicate where you want more bathrooms and bathtubs."

The practical decisions took a solid ten minutes to decide on a speculative basis. Balancing the historical cottage style with a modern B and B. When Ava felt like she had enough information to keep Jerome and his renovation crew busy, she introduced another topic. "I was thinking of putting together all my research and more interviews for a small, illustrated book about the lighthouse and the area. We could feature the lightkeeper's log written by Elizabeth Mayes in the 1920s."

"Marvelous!" Georgina gestured expansively. "I'll be your coauthor. And we absolutely must have a section about the Solomon family, starting with my great-great-grandpa George."

"At the same time, I could put together a historical display for the cottage, using the office with the wonderful rolltop desk."

"You know I expected to renovate that office into another bedroom for paying guests," Georgina said. "But I'll consider making it a historic setting."

"I think the Historic Landmark Board would appreciate the attention. And we could use the lightkeeper's logs for advertising."

"We'll see. Now, talk to me about schedules."

Ava pulled out a schedule with weekly goals and projects. "Right now, it's mostly demo and deconstruction."

"You've told me before, but what's the difference?"

"Demo is short for *demolition* and pertains to big jobs, like tearing out plumbing and replacing flooring."

"Like that god-awful linoleum in the kitchen."

"*Deconstruction* means taking things apart carefully, refurbishing them and replacing them. That's what we're going to do with the staircase so we can preserve the original carving." Ava introduced the topic of murder. "One of the subcontractors I've hired will need to take time off when the trial of Dr. Brody gets underway."

"Hasn't that proceeding started? Seems like we've been talking about it for weeks."

"It takes a while to gather evidence. What have you heard about the murder?"

"Not much. Stuart was cremated, you know. Wanted his ashes scattered at sea or some such nonsense. His mother and sister put together a memorial service that was poorly catered with few floral remembrances."

Harsh criticism. "I don't know the family. Are you close to them?"

"His mother never recovered from the humiliating divorce. Not Stuart's fault, of course, but she complains constantly about how none of the men in the family have properly supported her. Serena is much the same. Whining and moaning, she's furious that Stuart never changed his will and left his shares in the salvage business to his ex-wife and son."

"She never remarried, did she?"

"Hah! As a Donovan, you'd be among the first to know."

"Why?"

"Your brother Barry is the only man she's ever loved."

Ava's jaw dropped. She was shocked that Georgina Solomon knew gossip about her family. "I thought their relationship was over years ago."

"I've heard that the romance never really ended. Barry is quite handsome. He reminds me of that actor who plays a vampire in those movies set in Washington state."

"Really?" Her brother would hate the comparison.

"Of course, you wouldn't notice. You're his sister." Georgina casually studied the schedule. "When will you start working on the lighthouse tower?"

Ava dragged her attention back to the project at hand. "Not for a couple of weeks."

"That's what I'm excited about. I can't wait until the beacon is shining from the top of the lighthouse."

She wouldn't be too thrilled to know that Liam was currently hiding out in the lantern room. "I'm interviewing experts to repair the brick and stucco exterior."

"The damage can't just be painted over, can it?"

Ava took a deep breath and explained. When first built, the forty-eight-foot tower was pristine white, topped by polished glass, a metal widow's walk and a rotating beacon. Years of exposure had taken a natural toll, causing ragged chunks of stucco to separate from the bricks. Then came damage from Ava's nemesis—graffiti vandals. They marked the walls with garish scrawls and splattered paint without rhyme or reason. Their damage would require a great deal of work to erase or replace.

She heard a door slam in the rear of the house. "Company?"

"That's just Peter." Georgina raised her voice. "We're in here, sweetheart."

"Finally," Liam said. When Ava heard his voice in her ear, she jumped. Until now, he'd been silent, lurking in the woods and watching.

He continued, "You can stop talking about color swatches and actors playing vampires. Peter Quincy could be central to our investigation. Consider him a suspect."

Ava looked up as Quincy strode into the study. He didn't look like a killer. Quincy wasn't particularly attractive—not like her brothers or Liam—but he was well-groomed with light brown hair and a tidy goatee. His smile displayed perfect teeth. His forehead was smooth, unmarked by wrinkles. Blue eyes matched the color of his woven shirt with the sleeves rolled up to show his muscular forearms. When Peter Quincy married Georgina, who was eight years older, he fell into a great big pot of money, and he'd made good use of his fortune. He stepped up behind his wife's chair and leaned down to kiss her cheek.

She spread the color samples across the table in front of him. "Which do you like best?"

"They're all white."

She snatched up the one she'd chosen. "This one. Right?"

"If you say so." He nodded across the table. "Ahoy there, Ava."

In her experience, people who lived near the shore and used nautical language were either eighty years old or pretentious. She placed Quincy in the latter category. "Good afternoon."

While he sized her up, she saw a laser flash in the depths of his blue eyes. Either he considered her a threat or he didn't trust her. Either way, she'd be smart to heed the warning flare. Nervous, she broke eye contact and stared down at the notes, blueprints and color samples spread across the table. She might be imagining danger because of Liam's suggestion, but she didn't think so. Her survival instincts were usually reliable.

Forcing herself to meet his gaze, she tried to get the conversation rolling. Remembering Liam's advice, she said, "You two look happy together. How did you meet?"

Staying seated, Georgina gazed up at her husband. She laced the fingers of her left hand with his, and Ava noticed the gleam of her heavy, gold wedding band. Not as flashy as the diamonds worn by Holly Whitcomb in memory of her murdered husband but probably just as pricey. "You tell the story, sweetheart. You're more glib than I am."

Glib like a con man? Pasting an encouraging smile on her face, Ava listened to the story of Quincy spotting Georgina in Lincoln City during the November King Tide when the surf runs high. She was splashed by the spray of frothy waves crashing against the bridge, and he rushed forward to rescue her from the next onslaught. He pursued her relentlessly until she agreed to marry him.

"When I see what I want," he said, "I go after it. Nothing, and I mean nothing, stands in my way."

His single-minded determination worried Ava. What if Stuart had gotten crosswise with him? "Does the same attitude apply to your business?"

"I can be aggressive," he admitted.

"And he has quite the temper," Georgina said as she gazed up at him. "He's a deeply passionate man."

Ava cleared her throat and asked, "When were you married?"

"Five years ago in June," Georgina said. "I was thirty-seven and people in my family were already calling me a spinster. Can you believe it? So archaic. Don't you agree? You must be close to that age yourself, Ava."

"Twenty-seven."

"It's different in my family," Georgina said. "If I don't produce an heir, the purest branch of the Solomon bloodline will die out. Not really a valid concern. I have lawyers to handle inheritance issues."

Quincy added, "And now you have me."

"Anyway," Georgina continued, "I wasn't really looking for a husband. That's when Peter showed up."

"Good timing," Ava said, glad that her super-fertile sister and brother Jerome had already produced a batch of heirs if there had been any kind of Donovan fortune to pass down. "I hope Serena Whitcomb has that sort of good luck."

"Serena?" Quincy's smooth forehead creased. "What's her problem now?"

"You know," his wife chided. "She's not married and probably won't inherit her brother's shares in his salvage business."

"Either way, it's not a problem. I can work with Serena or with Holly. I'm sure either of those ladies will be happy to sell their half of Deep Dive to me."

In her ear, Ava heard Liam's calm but angry comment. "That bastard will never take over the business I built. If I go to jail, I'll sink every boat before I sell to him."

His hostility toward Quincy made sense to her. Georgina's husband was a competitor, and Liam didn't like to lose. Ava studied Quincy as he smoothed the neatly barbered hair on his chin. She said, "Sounds like you're planning to expand your operation."

"Sometimes, bigger is better." He grinned at Georgina. "Isn't that right?"

"I'm a fan of expansion."

"Don't get me wrong," Quincy said. "I liked Stuart, and he did okay with Deep Dive. But he wasn't a smart businessman, didn't take full advantage of the possibilities."

She had to wonder if he was talking about smuggling from Canada or fencing stolen artifacts from shipwrecks. "What about Liam?"

Quincy shook his head. "He's more interested in the discovery of shipwrecks. I could double or maybe even triple the profits."

His idea of taking over Deep Dive seemed hostile and creepy, but it didn't provide him with a motive for murdering Stuart. Quincy was a turkey vulture, diving down to pick at the bones of Stuart's livelihood. His plan to take over the business gave Quincy a reason to make sure Liam was convicted and spent the rest of his life in jail.

"My darling." Georgina gazed into his eyes. "Ava and I are

going to be writing a book about the lighthouse, and she needs to interview some of the locals. Who would you suggest?"

"Charlie Tancredo. He runs the Newport docks and his family has been here for a really long time." He gave his wife a peck on the cheek, stood up straight and stared at Ava. "I'm busy all day tomorrow but meet me Tuesday morning at Tancredo's office. I'm sure he'll have some stories to tell."

"I'll be there," she said.

Liam whispered into her ear. "Not by yourself. Too dangerous."

Ava agreed. Quincy or Tancredo or both of them could be murderers.

Chapter Twelve

As soon as Ava had dropped him off in the forest, Liam took advantage of the narrow, winding stream to wash off the stink of running, hiding and nearly suffocating in the trunk. He peeled off his jacket and shirt, wishing he'd thought far enough ahead to bring soap and toothpaste.

That was another instruction to include in his *Fugitive on the Run Handbook*. Also, he'd give obvious hints about evading the police, starting with how the good ones—like Marshal Woodburn—were always smarter than you expected. And how vital it was to have people you could trust like Ava. Using her as his touchstone, he could create a network from her family who would do anything to protect her. Also, there were former friends he could turn to. Maybe Fish Finley. Maybe Maxine Gallo. In his handbook, he'd devote an entire chapter to hygiene, starting with "Always be ready to wash yourself before you start to smell like roadkill."

Kneeling on a flat rock, he plunged both hands into the rushing water that came from snowmelt from Mount Hood and the Cascade Range. He gasped, splashed his face and gasped again. Too ice-cold to be considered refreshing, the shock quaked through his brain and got him thinking. Liam needed a plan to deal with newfound information.

Soon as possible, he'd establish a method of communicating with professional people who could dig deeper. Contacting his attorney or any possibly sympathetic law enforcement officer like Woodburn was out of the question. Their jobs obligated them to arrest him on sight and turn him in. His best bet was reaching out to Wyatt Willis, the private investigator he'd hired. The PI could set up an interview with Maxine Gallo and anybody else who would know about Stuart's unscheduled absences when he could have been smuggling or fencing salvage or showing Tancredo around the dive boat. Also, Willis might be able to figure out why Tancredo made that loan. What did Stuart have that was worth a quarter of a million?

Other issues revolved around drugs. Was there any truth to the rumors about Tancredo pushing prescription medication? If he had connections with drug smugglers from the northern border, was Quincy also involved? Were they a team? What about Oliver Whitcomb? Liam had spent time with Stuart's son when he was younger, but he barely knew the teenager. Much as he hated to think Oliver might have drugged him, the young man could be taking meds to deal with depression. He might be drug savvy. But why attack his old buddy Liam?

He shrugged back into his clothes while he listened to Ava's conversation with Georgina concerning bathroom fixtures and kitchen renovations at the cottage. Obviously, their designs wouldn't go back in time to the original 1890s stove and appliances, but Ava argued for blending modern upgrades with the retro-style of the early half of the 1900s.

Her self-control impressed him. Though she made her position clear, she listened to Georgina and treated her with kindness and respect. No doubt, Ava's life-long dealings with her large, contentious family gave her excellent negotiating skills.

He had taken a position at the top of the ridge overlooking Georgina's house when he heard Quincy enter and join the women. *Finally.* Liam hoped he'd hear details more relevant to the murder. At the same time, he'd noticed something or someone moving among the trees nearest the house.

Disguising himself behind the shadow of a moss-covered western hemlock, he watched as the shape took form. *Charlie Tancredo.* His grungy beige jacket and brown baseball cap blended with the surrounding forest. Tancredo crept through the trees, coming closer to the house and the office near the sun deck where Ava sat with Georgina and Quincy. In his left hand, the one with all the fingers, he held a handgun.

While listening through the earbud to Georgina chat about her first meeting with her adored husband, Liam watched Tancredo move closer with the stealth of a dark predator. What the hell was he doing? Threatening Ava? Or was he after Quincy?

Liam had guessed that Tancredo and Quincy were partners, but that assumption might be way off base. Through the earbud, he heard Quincy propose a meeting with Tancredo, who reacted to the mention of his name. He backed off and headed toward the road.

Inside the house, Ava was saying goodbye. Liam kept her in sight until she was safely behind the steering wheel of her Sonata and driving away from the house, then he bolted through the trees and down the hill, returning to their designated meeting spot. He got there just as she pulled over. Liam flung open the back door of the Hyundai and dove inside. Breathing hard, he said, "We've got to get away from here quick. You're not going to believe what I saw in the—"

"Yeah, yeah, tell me later. Right now, get in the trunk. I don't want to take a chance on anyone seeing you."

"Agreed." He pulled down the seat and hid himself in the

Hyundai's rear compartment but left one of the seats down. If anyone caught sight of Ava's car, they wouldn't see him, but he could still breathe. Claustrophobia had never been a problem for him in the past, and he figured these feelings of suffocation came more from his current helplessness than from a true psychological phobia. What the hell could he have done if he saw Tancredo take aim? Could he have stopped him? Being a fugitive meant he couldn't fight his own battles, couldn't even show his face. Until now, he hadn't been the sort of man who hid in the trunk and let others take risks.

When he thought of Ava facing Quincy and Tancredo at the marina without his protection, every muscle in his body tensed. He suppressed the urge to lash out, to punch something or…someone. Yes, he needed her help to investigate. But no, he refused to deliberately put her in danger. Her safety was a hundred times more important than the charges against him. If she were hurt or arrested, he'd be weighed down by a painful guilt that tortured him more than prison.

Through the earbud, she asked, "You heard what Quincy said, didn't you?"

"Yeah."

"He wants to acquire your business."

"Yeah, I heard."

When Quincy had been bragging about how he intended to take over Deep Dive, Liam had seethed. His search and salvage operation had never been designed as a profit-making endeavor. He and Stuart earned just enough money to cover expenses and minimal salaries, mostly because Liam chose their clients based on factors other than the final payoff. He and Stuart might have argued about the need to take on more jobs, but they agreed on the mission of their business: salvage, preservation and education. They didn't sell everything. Locked in the basement of his house, Liam stored several rescued objects that were waiting to be claimed by rightful owners.

When the Sonata emerged from the forest and drove onto a stretch of highway on the coast, he released some of his tension. The knot in his gut loosened, and he almost relaxed.

Through the back seat windows of the car, he watched the afternoon fade into twilight. A light rain began to fall. Ava lowered her window and inhaled the salty air. He saw her bend her arm and reach up into her thick, curly hair. "I'm taking out the earbud," she said.

"Fine with me."

"And unfastening the mic."

He did the same, slipping the small devices into his shirt pocket. More loudly than necessary, he said, "Can you hear me?"

"Of course, I can. You're shouting."

"You did a great job with Georgina. And earlier at Rachel's house. You've got a talent for investigation and interview."

"Thanks."

She sounded relatively happy. Much as he hated to burst her bubble, he said, "Tancredo was outside the house, watching through the window."

"What?"

"He had a gun."

"A gun? I can't believe it. He couldn't have been after me. I agreed to help him, to make his connection to you. As if that's ever going to happen. Was he after Quincy?"

Liam only heard every other word. Hearing her real voice with the window open was more difficult than their connection through the walkie-talkie. He wanted to talk things over with her but decided to wait until they could be face-to-face. "We'll talk about Tancredo later."

Ava took the turn leading into the Siuslaw National Forest. When they got closer to the lighthouse, he heard the coastal version of a watchdog—barking from the California sea lions mingled with cries from the gulls and nesting cormorants. The Sonata jostled along, circled the lightkeeper's cottage and aimed for the garage. At the big double doors, Ava jumped out to unfasten the latch and drove inside.

He emerged from the back seat, stretched and looked around the ramshackle barn. Enough light spilled inside through missing boards that he could clearly see the sit-down mower and two ATVs parked near the six horse stalls at the rear. Though the barn had been necessary in the early 1900s for housing the horses, hay and wagons, the building had outlived its purpose. Sooner or later, a decision would be made about whether to restore the barn or demolish it.

Ava pulled the door closed and approached him through the shadows. "Do I need to worry about Tancredo?"

"Short answer? Yes."

She drew a check mark in the air with her index finger. She was so cool, so casual that he had to be impressed. In a calm tone, she asked, "What about Quincy?"

"Should you worry about him? Oh, yeah." He hoped to convince her to ease off on her involvement in the actual investigating. "This is a major problem, Ava. Tancredo is obviously dangerous. He was creeping around with a gun in his hand."

"Why come after me?"

"He wants to get the money he loaned to Stuart. For some reason, he's decided that you know something about it."

"Doesn't make sense." She shook her head. "I barely knew Stuart."

"But you knew me. I was your professor way back when. You were the innocent, beautiful student. And I was the dirty old man."

She shot him a disbelieving glance. "You're only six or seven years older than I am."

"Six, but who's counting. Everybody in Narcissus is talking about you and me. Us." And he refused to be the reason she was threatened. "Tancredo thinks so. And that's why Quincy has a grudge against you. He came right out and said that he wanted to take over Deep Dive."

"Not fair," she said emphatically. "I'm getting blamed and shamed. And I'm not having any of the fun."

"Here's the thing," he said. "I'd appreciate your insights when we go over the new information you uncovered, but I don't want you physically involved in the investigation."

She shrugged. "I have a few objections. But okay."

"And I'm going to find another place to hide as soon as I can." He hated to leave, but he took a step away from her. "I'm going to go now. I'll add the new details to my notes."

She offered. "You can use my laptop."

"But I already have my computer set up in the lighthouse."

She tilted her head, gazed up at him and dropped the cordial mask he assumed she'd been wearing all day. A playful smile lifted the corners of her mouth making it look as though she had a secret. Her blue eyes sparkled. "Instead of your computer, we could use mine. You can stay in the cottage with me. We'll update the files together."

Much as he wanted to take her up on that offer, the stakes were too high. Not only was Deputy Jessop on red alert but her brothers were suspicious and Quincy might feel the need to check on her. If any of them found Liam in her house, she'd be in serious trouble. On the other hand, it didn't seem right to leave her alone and unprotected in the cottage. "I should go through the house with you right now. To make sure nobody's hiding inside."

"I didn't see any cars in the parking lot at the front or on the side." She yanked open the back door and started unpacking the stuff she'd brought with her. "I think it's okay. The main thing is to make sure nobody sees you. I want to avoid that nasty problem. I'm not a thrill seeker."

"I'm not talking about thrills. Swimming with sharks is a thrill. Confrontations with people—enemies and friends—are a whole different kind of risk."

"I get it," she said. "Humans are the worst."

"I've been thinking, Ava. We were lucky today. Nothing big went wrong, but we can't count on luck. There's no way I'm going to let you meet with Quincy and Tancredo by yourself."

"Excuse me?" She straightened her spine. Her teasing grin tightened into an angry line. "Did you really say that? You won't *let* me meet with them?"

"Those two guys are bad news. I don't want you to get hurt."

"I can make decisions for myself."

"I didn't mean to imply that you couldn't." Though he hadn't intended to provoke, her reaction was predictable. He had no right to tell her what to do, even though he was trying to protect her. Should he apologize? Would it do any good?

He reached toward her, gently touched her shoulder and allowed his hand to caress all the way down to her fingertips. "I have a better idea. For what we should do tonight."

She pushed his hand away and glared at him. "This better be good."

"We can work on my computer," he said. "In the lantern room at the top of the lighthouse."

"I'll do it."

Her answer had come quickly and impulsively. He'd expected more difficulty in calming her down but was willing to take the win. "Are you sure?"

"How could I say no? Ever since I came to Cape Absolute, I've wanted to see the view from the widow's walk. Sure, I could have dragged the ladder inside and figured a way to get up, but it seemed unnecessarily dangerous. Like I said before, I'm not a risk-taker."

"Give me fifteen minutes and come to the lighthouse."

"Make it forty-five," she said.

"Why?"

"It'll be sunset."

"You won't be disappointed. I've figured a good way for you to get up there."

She gave him a skeptical—but not outraged—look. "Are you promising a thrill ride?"

"You bet I am." He hoped that was a promise he could fulfill. Keeping her safe was all that really mattered.

Chapter Thirteen

Ava carried her cooler and other supplies toward the back door of the cottage. Though the sea lions and birds kept up their racket, she'd grown accustomed to their noise after living here for two and a half weeks. Her ears were attuned to any sound that might be unusual. The engine of a car or a motorcycle. A human-sized creature tromping through the forest. The whisper of conversation or the beep of a cell phone.

Likewise, she watched the play of light and shadow in the trees and down the hill toward the edge of the surf. She saw no sign that anyone was nearby, didn't sense the presence of a spy or an intruder. Still, she stayed alert. Liam was right to be concerned about someone staking out the cottage or spying on the lighthouse. Also right about the trouble that being observed could cause for both of them. She paid attention to what he said, but decisions were up to her alone. She would decide how involved she'd be in the investigation.

In the cottage, she carefully relocked the back door, dropped the leftovers in the kitchen and swept through the first floor, checking to see that no one had messed with the front door locks that hadn't been updated in the past thirty years. The entryway seemed okay, but papers on the rolltop desk in her office had been shuffled around. At least, she thought they were in different configurations. She remembered leaving a small yellow spiral notebook beside her computer. Or had she done that last night? Was she imagining the intrusion? Her laptop appeared to be untouched. Even if it had been turned on, she was password protected.

A floorboard creaked, and she looked in all directions, seeking the cause. The air was still. Silence surrounded her. *But I heard a sound.* And it rattled her. Groaning and scratching noises weren't unusual in an old house. Still, she reached for the lower desk drawer where she kept her pink Glock. Just as quickly, she pulled her hand back. Arming herself wasn't a rational idea. Even if Tancredo and Serena were packing pistols, Ava doubted her ability to defend herself with the Barbie-style Glock. To say the least, she wasn't a good shot.

If only Liam were here. Digging into her pocket where she'd put her earbuds and mic, Ava thought she could activate the walkie-talkie, but if he didn't have his receiver turned on, he wouldn't hear her. She stood very still, held her breath and listened. *Nothing.*

On high alert, she proceeded through the rest of the house and up the staircase to the second floor. Her suspicions might be nothing, but she worried. If an intruder accessed the sensitive information on her computer, they'd know she was working on the investigation into Stuart's murder.

Upstairs, she saw no sign of a disturbance until she entered her bedroom suite. In the center of her cream-colored chenille bedspread, she saw the yellow spiral notebook that belonged downstairs on the rolltop desk. *Left there as a warning.* Someone wanted her to find it. They wanted her to know she wasn't safe in the cottage. They could sneak inside. *I need to get the locks changed.*

She snatched the notebook, flipped it open. On the first page, in spikey handwriting she immediately recognized was a note: "Ava, you should get the lock on your front door upgraded."

Exactly what she'd been thinking. On the next page, he'd written: "I changed my mind about your boyfriend. No innocent man should go to jail. See you tomorrow A.M. I'll help."

Her knees gave out, and she collapsed onto the bed. Her brother had easily made his point by sneaking into her house and writing her a message. She really hoped he hadn't talked to the rest of the family about Liam. He wouldn't, would he? No way, Michael was smarter than that. Still…

She hit his cell phone number, and he answered immediately. "I picked your lock, Ava. It's amazing how many useful skills you pick up in prison."

"You scared me half to death."

"Good. That was my plan, sis. You need to take this seriously. Stuart was murdered, as in dead, and the person who did it is still out there, wandering around."

She was glad he agreed with her. "It wasn't Liam."

"I sure hope not because then I'd have to kill him for leading my sister on. And I don't want to go back to jail."

"See you in the morning," she said.

"I can come over tonight if you want."

"Not necessary."

She disconnected the call, rolled off the bed and shuffled into the bathroom. Tonight she intended to stay with Liam at the top of the lighthouse. This was their time. It might be their first, last and only chance to be alone. When she'd invited him to spend the night at the cottage, her motives hadn't been wholesome and innocent. From their brief kisses, he'd made it clear that he wanted more…and so did she.

She glanced in the mirror over the sink and groaned. The light rain had turned her naturally curly hair into a dark brown frizz ball, but her lips looked dried out. The mascara she'd been wearing at the beginning of the afternoon smudged down her cheeks. Repair work was necessary.

She jumped into the shower and washed away the nervous sweat of the afternoon. Clad in a towel, she worked a pinch of styling cream and a glob of mousse into her hair to control the curls. Then she padded barefoot through her bedroom to the closet. Somewhere in the back of her mind, she recalled Liam's favorite color was bright red. Or was it pink? She flipped through a selection of hanging shirts, finally selecting a soft coral blouse that buttoned up the front, making it easy to take off and display the lacy red bra she wore underneath. Since she'd be climbing around to get to the lantern room at the top of the lighthouse, she chose slacks in a chocolate brown that wouldn't show dirt. Completing her outfit were strappy, red sandals that were really more comfortable than they looked, plus the platforms added a solid four inches in height, which was always welcome for a shorty like her.

Checking her reflection in the old-fashioned full-length mirror in her bedroom, Ava decided she looked okay. Not glamorous unless she left the top three buttons of her shirt undone. But she was cute and ready for…something.

She glanced at her phone, wishing she could call her sister and ask for advice. Rachel was brilliant when it came to analyzing a relationship and figuring out what to do. What would she say about Liam? On the plus side, he was educated, financially solid and ruggedly handsome with a sexy smile. The big negatives were annoyingly obvious. He was charged with murder. And he'd skipped out on bail.

In the back of her mind, she heard Rachel's voice, speaking softly. She'd say, *You already know what you're going to do, Ava.*

"Do I?"

Follow your heart.

That would be Rachel's advice. And she would be one hundred percent right.

From the moment when Ava recognized Liam in the kitchen, she'd made up her mind that she wanted to act on the attraction she'd felt toward him when she was a student. They had chemistry. She trusted him, wanted to help him even if it messed up her career, and she instinctively believed in his innocence. Liam Brody wasn't a murderer. He was a good, decent man who needed her help to move forward with his life. Maybe, just maybe, she needed him as well.

In the kitchen, she refreshed Liam's supplies, making leftover meat loaf and cheddar sandwiches, selecting wine, adding fruit and more of her macadamia nut cookies to the insulated bag. She checked the vintage 1930s clock hanging over the back door. Time to go.

With the hood on her anorak flipped up, she hoped to preserve the minimal styling to her mop of hair. But when she stepped outside, the hood was unnecessary because the rain had stopped. The clouds thinned. Gulls and white-chested murres swooped through the skies to catch their last bit of food before the nocturnal hawks and owls took over on predatory night patrol. Again, she looked toward the forest and then to the shore, making certain she wasn't observed while she made her way across the fifty yards to the lighthouse.

Inside, Liam peered down through the hatch, thirty-seven feet above her head. "Fasten the bag to the rope. Just like before."

Following his instructions, she watched as their dinner and two bottles of Zinfandel ascended to the upper floor. After a pause, the rope slithered back down. Attached at the end was a triangular arrangement—a flat board about twenty-four inches wide fastened to the rope with nautical knots she recognized as Liam's handiwork. The contraption looked like a crude swing.

"Sit on the board and hang on," he said. "I'll pull you up."

Doubtful about this device, she asked, "Are you sure this is going to work?"

"You don't think I'm strong enough to lift you?"

She frowned. "I'm heavier than I look."

"This isn't about muscles. I've rigged a pulley system. Hop on."

Trying not to visualize herself in the hospital with two broken legs, Ava mounted the wooden swing. "I'm ready."

Her red platform heels swung off the floor. The curved walls of the lighthouse tower wrapped around her as she dangled, slowly ratcheting up a few feet at a time and swaying from side to side. The last time she'd been on a swing was years ago, and the sensation of weightlessness felt strangely titillating. He'd promised a thrill ride, after all.

Liam hauled her all the way up and through the rectangular hatch where he pulled her toward him. "Put your feet down," he said. "You're here. And you're taller."

"Platform heels." The short woman's best friend.

While he closed the hatch and fastened the bolts that held it in place, she looked around. They were standing in an enclosed, circular room where the mechanical equipment used to keep the light revolving were housed. A ledge ran below the windows. After it had been refurbished, the huge magnifying lens would be mounted in the center. Right now, before repairs, the space stood empty.

Liam had made himself at home. A sleeping bag spread out against one wall and a couple of crates served as chairs and tables. Smiling, he came toward her, caressed her cheek and tilted her head up toward him. "I have something I need to say."

"So do I." Light from the windows above them shone in his thick, dark hair and turned his gray eyes to silver. She mimicked his caress, gliding her fingertips down his cheek to the stubble on his chin. "You go first."

"I appreciate everything you're doing, and I trust you to make good decisions. At the same time, I've got to take a more active part. I can't spend these few days of freedom hiding in the trunk of your Sonata."

"I understand. But more involvement on your part sounds like a risk."

"For both of us," he said. "There are questions I need to ask. Fights I need to fight. You've done a great job of digging out gossip from the good people of Narcissus and getting me familiar with Georgina and her jerk of a husband."

"Stop." She placed her index finger across his mouth. "I'm not backing out. I need to be part of your investigation."

Outside, the wind whistled around the lighthouse. Liam took her to a narrow door and held it open for her. She stepped onto the metal widow's walk that encircled the top of the lighthouse. The heavy rain clouds lifted, and she gazed to the west. Skies of gold and red and magenta reflected in the rolling waves of the Pacific.

A good omen. Red sky at night. Sailor's delight.

Chapter Fourteen

Nothing stood between Ava and the sunset except a waist-high metal railing. She held tightly, anchoring herself. Perched near the top of the lighthouse, she was over forty feet off the ground on a cliff that towered another thirty feet higher than the shore. Behind her was the forest and the cottage. From where she stood on the widow's walk, she and Liam couldn't be seen, except by the birds and boats far out to sea. The horizon—lit by golden hues—rippled endlessly from north to south. Waves rushed toward the massive rocks below and crashed on the narrow, sandy beach in a mesmerizing rhythm.

Long ago, when she was a little girl, she imagined magical palaces where princesses danced all night in ornate ballrooms, and every day brought a new parade of exotic animals like elephants and tigers. The vast world spread before her, unlimited and exotic.

She glanced over her shoulder at Liam. "Is it safe to be out here in the open?"

"Facing the west, we're hidden. The lighthouse stands between us and the cottage. And the cliff juts out far enough that no one can watch from the forest."

"You've been out here before?"

"Late last night and early this morning. This is my first sunset." He placed the basket holding the food and wine she'd packed against the wall by the door and stood beside her at the railing. He stretched his long arm into the sky as though he could catch one of the soaring, swooping gulls. "When I'm at sea, this is my favorite time of day. The chores are done, and the sun goes down. Darkness settles, then comes the moon and stars. And I feel part of it all."

The glow from the sunset reflected on his face. A gust of wind swept his hair back from his forehead as he stared into the distance. He belonged out here with the sky and the surf. "Did you always want to be a sailor?"

"A swashbuckler," he said.

"And how did your parents feel about that occupation?"

When he shrugged off her question, she realized how little she knew about his background. And she needed to know. Last night, she'd thrown herself at him with very little real understanding of who he was, other than the obvious: handsome, intelligent and courageous. Also, she knew he came from wealth and grew up in the Pacific Northwest.

Once again, she probed. "Your mom and dad must have wanted something special for you when you grew up."

"We never talked about it. Not all families are like yours, Ava. My Brody kinfolk are among the crustiest of the upper crust. Most of them live back East. We're detached. I've met my aunts, uncles and cousins exactly three times, once at my mother's funeral. She died from a brain aneurysm when I was thirteen. My father was so wrapped up in his work as a virologist that he didn't have much inclination to spend time with me and my sister."

"I'm sorry."

"Can't complain," he said. "Nobody smacked me around or locked me in the basement. And they happily paid for just about everything I wanted. My sister runs the Brody Foundation based in San Francisco, and she organized the legal team for my defense."

"What about your father?"

"We haven't spoken."

"But you were arrested. You're facing trial."

"Not his problem." A thread of sadness wove through his words. "One thing I learned from him was to take care of myself."

She'd always envied rich people. Not anymore.

THINKING ABOUT HIS family curdled his blood. He refused to waste time worrying about his relationship with his father or, more accurately, the lack of one. His family history needed to stay in the past. Those distant relatives had never gone out of their way to hurt him. Well, maybe once or twice, but they weren't malicious. Brody family disagreements arose from financial conflict. *It's only business.*

He closed his eyes and leaned against the wall while those words repeated and echoed in his mind. He'd heard the voice before but couldn't identify the speaker. Once again, he flashed on that day on the yacht with Stuart. Lying helpless across the cushions in the stern near the dive deck, he tried to move but his limbs were too heavy. He struggled to open his eyes. Felt a shadow move over him. *It's only business.*

Clearly, he heard Stuart's voice. *Changed my mind.*

Forcing one eyelid to open, Liam managed to squint. Saw an inflatable boat bobbing in the water. The motor went silent. There were sounds of a scuffle.

As quickly as it had come, the vision vanished. Poof!

"Liam, are you all right?"

He gazed toward Ava outlined in the colors of the sunset. "I'm fine."

Too bad he couldn't use the memory fragments inside his

head as evidence. He needed proof, needed to know for sure that he wasn't a murderer. Only then could he seek a more fulfilling commitment with Ava.

He wrapped his arm around her slender waist and pulled her close. Her nearness warmed him. In her tall wedge sandals, the top of her head came up to his chin. They fit together very well. Her curves pressed into his body, filling the empty spaces. The sweet, clean fragrance of her hair teased his nostrils, and he was glad he'd taken the time for an ice-cold bath in the forest so he'd smell more like pine resin than sweat. He wanted to be even closer to her, to taste her lips and feel her breasts rubbing against his chest. Her invitation to stay in the cottage tonight became a serious temptation, even though he knew the timing was wrong for them to sleep together in a desperate act of passion. He couldn't help wondering if her sheets were satin and her mattress was firm and her nightgown was filmy. So tempting but not yet.

"I'm lucky to have such a loving family," she said, picking up the conversation they'd dropped before the scattered remnants of his vision interrupted. "True, they drive me up the wall, but they're as much a part of me as my ears or my arms."

"Or your heart." Liam reined in his desires. Right now, he needed to be smart, logical and focused on their investigation. "You mentioned you had something to tell me."

"Don't be mad," she said.

"What is it?"

"Remember that loving family we were just talking about? Well, sometimes they overstep and stick their noses where they don't belong." Her shoulders rose and fell as she huffed a sigh. "Michael broke into the cottage while we were at Georgina's house. He swiped a notebook off my desk and took it upstairs to the bedroom where he left a note telling me to upgrade my lock on the front door."

Not happy about her brother's intrusion, he asked, "What does he want?"

"He's had second thoughts about you and wants to help. The note said it's not right for an innocent man to be incarcerated, and Michael knows from personal experience what that particular brand of injustice feels like."

"Does he know I'm with you?"

"I haven't told him, but he suspects. He wants to meet tomorrow morning, and I'd like to introduce you. Your decision, Liam. What do you say?"

He hesitated for a moment while pluses and minuses balanced on a scale. The possibility of pluses won. "I say welcome aboard. We need all the help we can get."

"I'm not sure what he can do."

"We'll think of something." He already had a good idea how the presence of Michael Donovan could solve the problem of having Ava face Quincy and Tancredo at the Port of Newport. Michael could accompany her. Those two wouldn't dare threaten her while her tough, ex-con brother protected her.

"You'll like him," Ava said with unshakable certainty. "You and Michael remind me of each other. You're both loners, both tough guys—"

"Bad boys?"

She nodded. "The main difference is that you're a sailor, and he's a cowboy. After his release from jail, he moved to Pendleton where he works on a ranch. Do you like horses?"

"I went to the Kentucky Derby once."

She chuckled. "I'll have to take you to the Pendleton Round-up in September. It's one of the oldest rodeos in the country."

Her comment surprised him. Making plans for the future?

Their future together? Somehow, in spite of all the suspicion and doubt, she believed he wouldn't be in prison and they'd still be with each other. He wished he had her confidence.

After a quick kiss, he separated from her, took a step forward, looked over the railing and pointed to the cliff below. "That looks like a path going all the way down to the shore."

She joined him and leaned out so far that he was compelled to grasp her arm above the elbow. No fear of heights from Ava. "Looks different from this perspective. It's a narrow, rocky trail. Not a terribly difficult descent, it comes out on the beach not far from Seal Rock. From there, it's a short walk to the dock."

"The dock?" He brightened. "I can't see a dock from here."

"It's tucked under the cliff, well protected from incoming surf."

"Do you have a boat?" He'd welcome a way to move around the coast without hiding.

"Not even a canoe."

The dock couldn't be seen from the cottage or from the edge of the cliff. Not a bad place for a secret meeting. Tomorrow morning, he could talk to Fish Finley on that secret shore after Fish arrived for work at the cottage. Liam brightened at the thought of investigating outdoors instead of hiding in secret passageways, trunks of cars and the isolated room at the top of the lighthouse. "I know Fish has a little motorboat."

"He's come to work by sea a couple of times." She frowned. "You aren't thinking of talking to Fish, are you? He's testifying for the prosecution. Not on your side."

"We'll see." Liam shifted to another branch of their inquiry. "When you were with Georgina, you noticed her cuff bracelet. Did you snap a photo?"

"Got it right here." She dug into the pocket of her anorak and took out her phone. Before she showed him the bracelet, Ava turned to the west and snapped a succession of photos capturing the golden sunset below the dark purple clouds. Then she handed over the phone and sat with her back leaning against the whitewashed wall below the beacon windows. She pulled the basket with food and wine closer and reached inside.

Liam concentrated on the screen that displayed a three-inch gold cuff with an intricate Deco design featuring rows of pyramids alternating with curlicue roses. "Expertly cleaned up. You can still see the detail."

"That's correct, Professor. In class, you told us that gold coins and jewelry retrieved from shipwrecks suffer less deterioration than most other metals. I've used that rationalization to always buy gold jewelry."

"This pattern is similar to goods we salvaged from a merchant ship that sank in the 1920s. Quincy gave this to his wife, right?"

She nodded.

"The property from this salvage operation was returned to the owners of the ship and their insurance company. And Deep Dive was paid a substantial fee for the find." He looked from the screen of her phone to the brilliant sunset, hoping there might be an innocent reason for Quincy to have this bracelet. "I hate to think Stuart took this bracelet from our inventory and gave it to his buddy."

"I can't believe that would happen," she said. "Don't you keep records of artifacts?"

"Of course." And Stuart kept the records. Detailed records, written by hand and entered into the computer. "I trusted him."

"Where do you store the objects you salvaged?"

"Some are in my basement. Others are kept in a secure warehouse."

"How secure?"

Some of the objects they found were valuable, like the bracelet Quincy had given to his wife. A high level of security was required, and Liam had been using this warehouse for years, ever since he made significant finds in the Strait of Juan de Fuca. The space was temperature controlled and windowless with locks on the area belonging to Deep Dive and also at the entrance where guards were on duty day and night.

"Very secure," he said. "The only ones with access are me and Stuart. Once a year, we take inventory."

"Comparing the objects in storage against Stuart's listings."

"When I was arrested, the police checked the warehouse. They found nothing missing."

She suggested, "Maybe because Stuart never wrote things down in the first place."

I'm a fool. He cursed himself for believing in his partner and not taking the time to have an independent third party record their inventory. "Stuart must have given the bracelet to Quincy in exchange for... I don't know what."

"Doesn't matter," she said. "It's evidence that Stuart and Quincy were in cahoots."

"Cahoots? Who are you? Some kind of noir detective like Sam Spade?"

"I used the word correctly. It implies a partnership for nefarious purpose, and I like the way it sounds. Cahoots. Cahoots."

He smiled as he returned her phone, but his anger and disappointment didn't fade. In a quiet voice, almost as though he was talking to himself, he said, "I didn't want to believe that Stuart was cheating me. But here's proof. He gave or sold this piece to Quincy. And he invited Tancredo onto the dive boat when I wasn't on board."

"Sorry," she said.

"We'd been partners for eight years and friends for longer than that. I remember when he got married and when his son was born. I crewed on his yacht, and I thought Stuart was amazing."

"We all make mistakes," she said as she lifted out a bottle of Zinfandel and showed him the label. "From a Willamette Valley winery."

"I like a good red."

"I thought you might." She whipped out a corkscrew. "Growing up, I didn't know Stuart well, but he had a reputation in Narcissus for cheating and lying and going through a new girlfriend every week. Stuart's sister hated her brother's infidelity and compared him to my brother Barry."

"Serena, right? The woman with the gun in her purse."

"Sticky Serena the Human Saran Wrap, that's what my sister called her because she was clingy. Rachel didn't much care for Stuart, either. I remember how furious she was when Holly told her she was pregnant."

"Are you saying your sister didn't approve of an unmarried pregnancy?"

"Nothing so close-minded. Rachel expected Stuart to break Holly's heart, and she didn't want her friend to be hurt."

"Was she right?"

"Not at first." Ava handled the corkscrew with easy expertise to open the bottle with a subtle pop. "Right after they got married, Holly lived the life of an Oregonian princess in a sprawling mansion with a full-time maid and a chef. Stuart took her on a trip to Europe, then to the Bahamas and he was totally gaga over his baby boy."

She took two plastic wineglasses from the basket, handed

them to him and poured the glistening, red liquid. Ava held up her glass for a toast. "To innocent men."

"And the women who believe in them."

The wine tasted of cherries, earth and spice. The flavor aroused his palate. Liam wasn't much of a drinker, but he liked his wine.

Ava made a yum noise that was unintentionally sexy. "Anyway," she said, "Holly had a happy ending for a while."

"Few and far between."

In his experience, "happily-ever-after" only occurred in the endings of rom-com movies. He turned his head and gazed into her big beautiful blue eyes. He'd gladly settle for "happy right now."

When he inclined toward her, she tilted her chin to receive his kiss. The last golden rays from the setting sun warmed them and drew them closer. He set his wineglass down and reached for her. This kiss required both hands. With one, he traced the ridge of her spine down her back to the fullness of her hips. The other hand slipped inside her coral shirt. When his fingers touched her bare torso, she gasped and gave a wiggle that encouraged him to reach higher and brush his fingertips against the soft, delicate underside of her breast. Another quick intake of breath. Her skin felt hot and smooth. Still balancing her wine, she shifted position until she was sitting on his lap with one arm coiled around his neck.

She nuzzled his throat, nipped at his earlobe and kissed his cheek. "You're fuzzy," she whispered.

"And you're satin."

He kissed her again, tasting the earthy flavor of the Zin. She threw back her head and downed the rest of her wine in one glug. In a carefree gesture, she tossed away her plastic glass and slanted her lips across his. The kiss was hard, passionate. She drew him into her until he was drowning, happily abandoning any pretense of intelligence or logic.

The raucous cries of gulls had faded at the end of day, and the gentle murmur of the surf serenaded them. Their high perch on the widow's walk, facing toward the ocean and away from the cottage, kept them safe from observation. No one could see them but the diving, swooping birds. They were alone in a private, intimate world.

But they weren't.

The world hadn't stopped turning. He was still a fugitive, accused of murder and looking at a life behind bars. In spite of the fierce urge to make love to her right here, right now on the widow's walk, he needed to regain control. If he didn't get them back on track with the investigation, he'd lose his ability to make sense of the evidence. *I don't want to go to jail.*

Summoning every ounce of willpower, he lifted her off his lap and set her down beside him. She gasped for breath. Her cheeks flushed bright red. Regretfully, he said, "We can't."

Though her gaze turned as predatory as a blue-eyed tigress, she agreed. "Certainly not."

"I need to update my data."

She bounded to her feet. "I'll get your laptop."

Good thing she didn't expect him to move quickly. It'd take a few minutes before he was able to stand.

Chapter Fifteen

The next morning at half past seven, Ava tried not to think of her dream deferred and unfulfilled. Last night, she'd imagined that her budding relationship with Liam would blossom to a more intimate level—a nice way of saying she wanted to have sex with him. But he'd sidestepped her obvious advances. In retrospect, she told herself she ought to be glad. If they waited until his future was more secure, they might have a chance at something deeper and more serious than a frantic, one-night coupling. Already, she'd waited six years for him to notice her. A few more days were no big deal.

She left the cottage while the blushing sunrise colored the skies above the giant boulders close to shore and the incoming tide. With her earbuds and mic in place, she spoke to Liam when she reached the path leading down to the rugged, sandy beach. "Are you sure it's safe for you to come outside?"

"Nothing is a sure thing, but I'm ready to give it a try."

Still, she couldn't dismiss the ever-present threat from Jess-hole and the manhunt she'd heard about on the news last night. The TV reporters made Liam sound like a mad-dog supervillain, but the accompanying photo showed a handsome hero, which somehow made him more horrible in a Jekyll-and-Hyde sort of way. Hiding in secret places hadn't been easy for him, but stepping into the light could be worse. "It's risky."

"I'll meet you at the dock under the cliff."

Climbing down the path, she picked her way through rocks, beach grass and prickly shrubs to the hard-packed sand where a couple of sea lions waved to her from their long, flat rock near the breaking waves. Her descent took only a few minutes. At the bottom, she gazed up at the lighthouse towering like a beacon of hope. An unlit beacon. How appropriate for her current mood!

Standing at the edge of the water with morning sunlight dancing on the waves, she turned her head and watched him hike down the hillside. As soon as his boots hit the sand, he strode toward her with long strides, wrapped his arms around her and nuzzled her earlobe. His two-day growth of stubble scratched her cheek. He whispered, "I like being out here with you. With the wind and the waves…"

"And the squawking gulls." She stepped out of his embrace, grasped his hand and pulled him toward the overhanging cliff where the short dock bridged over the water. "We're not safe yet. We need to make ourselves less obvious."

"Fine by me."

"Michael is going to meet us here around eight o'clock, which means he could arrive at any moment." She took out her earbuds and deactivated the mic. "What have you been doing this morning?"

"I followed up on a call I made last night to Wyatt Willis, the private investigator I used before. He'll do some poking around. His first project is locating Maxine Gallo."

"The assistant," she remembered.

"I have some specific questions for her about the inventory of salvage we've collected and stored at the warehouse." He removed his earbuds and mic. "I also have questions about Stuart's shares in our partnership."

"And you need to know what happens to Deep Dive if you're convicted and go to jail."

He cringed. "Don't remind me."

She didn't regret her words. He needed to keep the stakes in mind. "What are you going to talk to my brother about?"

"Anything he might know about Holly, Ollie and Serena."

"They sound like a trio of folk singers."

"Mellow." He walked past her to the short wooden dock where no boats were moored. "I like this tiny marina. Did it get a lot of use when they were first building the lighthouse?"

"Not really, large ships or tall sailboats wouldn't try to maneuver through these rocks. This is more of a dinghy dock." She grinned. Being outdoors with him made her cheerful in spite of the danger. "What do you want Michael to find out about the threesome?"

"Why does Holly still wear her wedding ring when she's been divorced for years? How much does Oliver know about the drug scene in Narcissus? If Serena inherits her brother's share of Deep Dive, what is she going to do with it?"

Ava frowned. Michael wasn't a particularly social person, definitely not a gossip like her sister. "You might be asking the impossible. Michael isn't a chatty guy. And if he approaches Serena, she might glom onto him as a substitute for my other brother Barry."

"Mostly, I want your big, strong brother to act as your bodyguard."

She scoffed. "I'm not in danger."

"Tell that to Jessop when he threatens you."

Irritated, she stalked toward the dock and slapped the top of a waist-high, rugged piling. "I can handle Jess-hole."

"With your little pink Glock?" He walked to the end of

the dock and peered into the water. "To tell the truth, I'm more worried about Tancredo and Quincy."

"Quincy was quick to suggest I talk to Tancredo as a source for local legends," she said. "Why else would they want to meet with me?"

"To find out what you know about me and about Stuart's murder," he said. "I don't trust those guys, and I'd feel a hell of a lot better if your brother stood at your side."

She had to admit that Michael had an intimidating aura. After spending years in prison, he'd developed a flat, menacing stare that could look right through you. Without speaking a single word, he conveyed ice-cold intensity. "Okay, Liam. I'm guessing you have another theory about the murder. Let's have it."

He shrugged. "I need confirmation from the PI, but I've heard that Tancredo has connections for fencing illegal salvage."

"Like Georgina's gold bracelet."

"And Newport is a natural location for smuggling."

"So you think Quincy and Tancredo were in cahoots with Stuart." Under her breath, she repeated the ridiculous word. "Cahoots, cahoots."

"Here's my theory. Stuart invited me out for a boat ride to get me alone. He drugged me with some nearly untraceable concoction that he got from Tancredo."

"Why?"

"Tancredo had loaned Stuart a bunch of money and wanted to get it back. To do so, Stuart needed to get me out of the way so he could take over Deep Dive and expand into the illegal salvage business with Quincy."

"Wait." She held up both hands to stop his narrative. "I like this theory better than your idea about Stuart and Ollie drugging you. This time, you think Stuart intended to murder you so he could make more money. Doesn't track because the Whitcomb family is loaded. For that matter, Quincy married wealth. He's not hurting."

"Greed is an interesting phenomenon," he said. "What most people consider filthy rich, others find lacking. Stuart might have wanted more. The same goes for his sister."

"The upper crust," she murmured.

"Back to my theory." He gave a professorial gesture. "I was unconscious on the boat with Stuart at the helm. Quincy boarded, probably using an inflatable boat. Instead of killing me, they argued. Quincy is famous for his bad temper. In a rage, he whacked Stuart and killed him."

"Which leaves him adrift in the ocean with one dead man and another unconscious."

"Thinking on his feet, Quincy tosses the murder weapon overboard and leaves, knowing the police will assume I'm the killer and will end up in jail."

She hated to admit that he might have solved the mystery without her help and focused on the part of his theory that still seemed off-kilter. "How does Quincy profit from Stuart's death and your incarceration?"

"I don't have that part worked out." Liam stepped off the dock and onto the sand. He peered into the shadows from the cliff. "What do you think, Michael? Any ideas?"

Ava watched her brother emerge from the dark and come toward them. What was going on here? She hadn't told her brother that Liam was sleeping in the lighthouse. Her plan had been to introduce them and carefully evaluate whether these two volatile men would be able to work together without exploding. Only then would she admit to a relationship with the fugitive.

Michael had taken that choice away from her. Somehow, he'd crept down here without being seen. Or maybe he'd arrived early and had been waiting for them, confident that they couldn't hear his approach over the rustling of the surf, the screams of the birds and the barking sea lions.

"Back off, Michael." She snarled at him. "Why are you here so early?"

He barely glanced at her. His hard-edged gaze rested on Liam as he came closer. Somehow, he managed to not look clumsy walking across the sand in his pointy-toed cowboy boots. He halted a few feet away. "Answer my sister's question. How does Quincy profit?"

"My guess? He needs help from Serena."

"Yeah," Michael said, "that's the way I'd call it."

Ava glared at one, then the other. Neither Liam nor her brother cracked a smile. A well-matched pair, both stood over six feet tall. Both were lean with wide shoulders and narrow hips. Liam's hair was darker, but he and Michael both had angular features and stubborn jaws. If they worked together, they'd be formidable. If not…

"I don't understand." She threw up her hands in surrender. "How can Serena help Quincy?"

Liam kept his focus on Michael while he answered her. "In spite of being detail oriented, Stuart never changed his will when he divorced Holly two years ago. The way it's set up now, his son inherits his estate—properties, investments, trust funds and tangible purchases. Holly is appointed to act as trustee and executor. He split his 49 percent ownership in Deep Dive between his son and his sister. Serena wants it all."

"I'm still confused," Ava said. "I don't understand how Quincy fits in."

Liam explained. "In addition to being greedy, the upper crust sticks together. I'm guessing that even though Serena and Georgina don't like each other, they'll work together for profit.

Quincy can manipulate both of them. Serena doesn't want to run Deep Dive. Once she has all of her brother's shares, she can sell them for an inflated price to Georgina's husband. Combining Deep Dive and his own salvage business makes Peter Quincy the main guy in that business for central Oregon."

"He's right." Michael nodded like a handsome cowboy bobblehead. "You're not as dumb as you look, Brody."

"He's a PhD," she said. "Of course, he's intelligent."

"Now isn't a time for book smarts, little sis. We need street smarts, and the ability to think like murderers and criminals."

"There's one more piece to this theory," Liam said. "In order for Serena's minority ownership to be useful, Quincy still needs to get me out of the way. Another murder would be suspicious. But if I go to jail..."

He left the thought hanging and Michael finished it. "In jail, you couldn't interfere with their plans."

"Exactly."

When Liam reached out for a handshake, Michael stared at his fingers for a long five seconds before accepting the gesture. Expecting them to be friends was too much, but Ava hoped they'd be able to work together.

AFTER AVA AND her brother Michael hiked up the path to the cottage to meet the work crew headed by her other brother Jerome, Liam got comfortable in the shadows under the cliff. He'd brought along his laptop in his backpack but didn't take it out. Last night, he'd spent too many hours hunched over his computer, honing his theory and trying not to think about how much he'd rather be sharing his makeshift lighthouse bed with Ava. He sprawled, kicked off his boots and dug his toes into the sand. A dose of sun and surf would help him regain his balance before his meeting with Fish Finley.

He intended to deny any affiliation with Ava or her brothers, but his mere presence near the lighthouse made the connection. Even Fish—who wasn't the swiftest guppy in the tank—could draw that obvious conclusion. What would he do with that information? What were the odds that he'd support Liam?

On the plus side, he and Fish had developed a comfortable work relationship over the years. With Deep Dive, Fish earned a decent hourly wage plus overtime and insurance benefits, even though he was part-time. After a dive, Fish came along with the rest of the crew for beer and burgers. He was friendly. And loyal.

And yet, he'd agreed to testify for the prosecution. That was the minus. If this conversation turned out wrong, Fish might report to Deputy Jess-hole. Why? Either he secretly hated Liam or he intended to sell the information to the highest bidder. Most likely, the latter.

Might have been smarter and safer to call Fish on the phone for this chat, but Liam wanted personal contact. When he and Michael Donovan confronted each other in person, they created a more intense bond. No guarantee they wouldn't argue in the future. But they shook hands and silently pledged trust. It was understood that they both wanted whatever was best for Ava. He hoped to make the same kind of connection with Fish.

He stood and stretched, brushed off the sand and strolled to the dock. At the end he sat and dangled his bare feet in the cold water. As the sun rose higher in the skies, a gang of dark brown California sea lions lolled in the sun, flapping their fins and occasionally barking. The spotted harbor seals—less sociable creatures—glared and ignored their whiskered cousins.

Liam had a couple of strategies in mind.

First: if the meeting went well, Fish might be convinced to come to work tomorrow at the lighthouse on his motorboat. Having water transport and diving equipment opened up all kinds of possibilities. Using the water, Liam had a way to follow Ava and Michael to the docks in Newport and avoid being seen.

Strategy number two: if Fish had been paid for his testimony, Liam could double the cash involved to make sure Fish would be on his side.

Number three: a long-term goal for Fish—especially since he was starting a family—might be to have permanent employment. Liam could offer that. With Stuart gone, he was shorthanded at Deep Dive and salvage jobs were piling up.

A trio of sea lions slipped into the water and glided to the beach where they waddled at the edge of the breaking waves and made noise. Liam took their performance as an announcement that Fish was on his way down the path. Leaving the dock, he returned to the sandy beach but didn't put his shoes on.

Though he'd seen Fish less than two months ago, there was a significant change in the skinny young man with the shaved head and the pouty lips outlined by a scruffy goatee. His shoulders were high, and his backbone stiffened. He wasn't smiling.

Liam approached and held out his hand. "Thanks for showing up."

Fish gripped, shook and released. His gaze was unwavering. "I didn't tell Bonnie I was going to see you. I'm pretty sure she wouldn't like it."

"Bonnie is your fiancée," Liam said, grateful that Fish hadn't spread the news about their meeting to anybody else. "Congratulations."

"We're going to have a baby."

"Congrats, again."

"I'm pretty sure she'd want me to turn my back and walk away. But Ava is my boss's sister, and I can't afford to lose this job."

"Money is tight. I get it."

"Do you know how much diapers cost? And car seats and cribs and formula. Man, it's a small fortune. And Bonnie wants a house with three bedrooms—one for us, a nursery and a home office for her so she can do her crafts and her podcasts."

If Fish went unchecked, he'd continue to babble like an artesian spring. Liam rested his hand on the younger man's shoulder and said, "Maybe I can help."

"What do you mean?"

"Suppose somebody offered you a payment in return for your testimony. Not saying that's what happened. This is hypothetical."

Fish pursed his pouty lips and nodded. "Suppose they did."

"Why do you think they'd do that?"

"They're out to get you, Brody. They might have offered me four thousand bucks. In a hypothetical way. And I'm not going to lie. You and Stuart argued. All the time."

"I've got a temper," he admitted, but there was a big difference between an argument and a death threat. "What did you overhear?"

"You were fighting about safety procedures. As usual." Fish had an unusual way of chuckling, expelling small bursts of air in a glug-glug-glug noise. "You're always on us about bringing along newbies or checking our air gauges."

Which was why Liam bought health insurance for all his employees and required them to have regular checkups to make sure they were fit to dive. "I'm a safety-first kind of guy."

"Don't I know," Fish said. "Anyhow, you told Stuart that

the next time he ran his tank too low you wouldn't help him out, wouldn't haul his ass back into the boat."

"Do you think I meant it? Really? Do you think I'm a murderer?"

"Hell, no."

"Why are you testifying against me?"

Fish shrugged his narrow shoulders. "This is still hypothetical, right?"

"Sure."

"I might have agreed on account of I'm desperate for cash. What's the harm? Everybody knows you're not a killer. No way will you be convicted. I mean, they let you out on bail."

"Who gave you the money? Hypothetically."

"Everybody speaks well of you, man. You've got a sterling reputation."

"I want a name, and I'll pay you double the hypothetical four thou."

"Serena Whitcomb. That's eight thou, right?"

Chapter Sixteen

Liam couldn't claim to be surprised. Learning that Serena Whitcomb had paid Fish to testify for the prosecution fit neatly with his reasoned-out theory of the murder. Serena would do anything in her power to make sure Liam went to prison and lost control of Deep Dive.

He gave Fish a nod. "I appreciate your honesty."

"It's all I can do. Can't perjure myself." He puffed out his cheeks and tried to look solemn. "I won't tell a lie on the witness stand. I heard you and Stuart arguing, but I also know you didn't mean any real harm. Like when you get really mad and tell somebody that you're going to take them out into the middle of the ocean, tie them to an anchor and feed them to the sharks but before you do…"

Fish was off and running with one of his long-winded monologues, leaving Liam to wonder about Serena's motives. How could she agree to Stuart's murder? *Not a good look for the rich lady.* But Quincy might have explained his assault on Stuart as an accident, a result of losing his temper and lashing out. Liam cut into Fish's narrative which showed no sign of slowing. "Does Serena think I killed her brother?"

"Who can tell?" He gestured helplessly. "Underneath all her fancy clothes and polish, she's a nervous woman. Changes her mind every ten seconds."

"Did you know she carries a gun in her purse?"

"Hell, no. I don't like that. Not at all."

Liam moved on to his final strategy of satisfying a long-term goal for Fish. "I want to offer you a full-time job at double the salary I was paying before. You start right now."

"But nothing's going on with Deep Dive."

"This isn't about scuba," he said. "I need an executive assistant."

"An executive, huh? Bonnie is going to like the way that sounds."

"But you can't tell her." Liam's voice was firm. "If you take the job, that's your first assignment. Don't tell anybody that we talked, and you're working for me. Can you do that?"

"You got it, boss." Fish gripped his hand and gave a vigorous shake. Though skinny, he had surprising strength. "Can I still work for Ava's brother on construction?"

"I wouldn't have it any other way."

Liam took out his wallet and pulled out five hundred-dollar bills. Another tip for his *Fugitive on the Run Handbook*: always carry cash, lots of it. "Here's a signing bonus. Now you work for me."

"Fair enough." The cash disappeared into his back pocket. "You're sweet on cute, little Ava, aren't you?"

"I am. But don't tell her. Or her brothers."

"I'll keep a lid on it."

Fish was strong, loyal and oddly perceptive. Couldn't ask for more in an assistant. For maybe the first time since he'd been arrested, Liam felt like he was in control of the situation. "Here's your first assignment. Ava mentioned your motorboat and said you sometimes use it to come to work."

"Not today," Fish said. "I took my Yamaha motorcycle because Bonnie needed the car."

"Tomorrow, bring your boat and moor it right here at this

dock." He would arrange for them to motor over to Newport and keep an eye on Ava's meeting with Quincy and Tancredo. "Can you do that?"

"Aye, boss."

Liam liked the way they'd fallen into their usual relationship. He was the captain, and Fish was the crew. "Better idea. Can you take off at lunchtime, go home, get your boat and bring it back here?"

"Aye."

He wished his mic and earbud were active so he could tell Ava about his plan. They were another step closer to finding the truth. As if the mere thought of her had conjured her presence, he looked up and saw her running across the beach toward them.

AVA HADN'T WANTED to interrupt his conversation even though she expected it to go well. Like everybody else in town, Fish knew she and Liam were connected. When she told him that he needed to hike down to the shore near Seal Rock because someone wanted to see him, the first words out of his mouth were, *Brody. It's Liam Brody, right?*

She couldn't come up with a plausible denial, so she'd said nothing and smiled.

Fish smiled back.

From the casual look of the two men near the short dock, they seemed to be getting along. She hoped so because she was about to drop another bombshell. When she reached Liam, she gasped for breath. "It's Ollie," she said. "On his way."

"Here?" he asked.

"Yeah." Stuart's son had sounded angry over the phone. Now wouldn't be the best time to test the waters and find out how the teenager felt about Liam. "You need to step back into the shadows."

"That's probably wise."

She caught her breath and turned to Fish. "Did everything work out for you?"

"I'm an executive, but you can't tell anybody. Bonnie is going to be happy. So, yeah, I'm happy."

"I'm glad, Fish." Later, she'd catch up on the details. "I'd like for you to return to the cottage. Jerome has a project for you."

"You got it, Ava. And thanks." He dashed toward the path leading up the cliffside, waving a greeting to the curious, dark brown sea lions as he passed. They responded with raucous barking.

She whirled to face Liam, placed her palms flat against his chest and pushed him toward the cliff into the rock-strewn darkness where Michael had hidden. "Ollie suspects that I know where you are. He wants me to give something to you, says it's important."

"What is it?"

"He didn't tell me. And he's got to talk to you before his aunt Serena finds you."

"Am I missing something?" He stepped into the shade. "How is everybody figuring out that I'm here?"

"Small town osmosis. One person wonders. Another speculates and tells another. Pretty soon, the entire population of Narcissus is talking about how I'm harboring a fugitive." She didn't like the way things were turning out. "It's only a matter of time before we have another hostile visit from Woodburn and Jess-hole."

"Maybe I should meet with Ollie while I can." His smile bloomed with confidence. She could tell that something inside him had changed. "I'm encouraged by how well the talk with Fish went."

"Fish likes you. He knows you're a decent person."

"Am I? Because I keep having indecent thoughts about you and me."

Hidden under the cliff, the shadows spread around them and masked them from view and she felt safe enough to glide into his warm embrace. The cool sea breeze swirled around them. His lips tasted of sun and salt. She had to step back before her own indecent urges overwhelmed the need for caution. She cleared her throat. "What kind of relationship do you have with Ollie?"

"I've known the kid since he was born, literally. While he and Holly were still in the hospital, I visited and gave him an infant-sized sailor cap. When he was older, I took him trick-or-treating. Went to his Little League games."

"What about his teen years?" She thought of the foundations and charities where Liam volunteered. She knew that he sponsored trips for at-risk kids and also taught boating, swimming, fishing and snorkeling. "You seem to get along well with adolescents. Some people might say it's because you never grew up."

"What would you say?"

She avoided that touchy subject. Her long-held opinions about how rich kids were raised with too many advantages and too few responsibilities weren't really fair and ought to be kept to herself. "Tell me about Ollie. Were you 'good, old Uncle Liam'?"

"I hope not. He was a smart kid, and I never talked down to him. We were close. But when he was a teen, we grew apart." He spread his palms and gestured helplessly. "I didn't know what to do. Stuart and Holly were having problems, which were none of my business. But I felt bad for the kid, wanted to offer support."

"Did you tell him that?" she asked.

"I took him fishing, and we'd sit on the boat. We'd be mostly silent for hours."

"Is taking care of Ollie how you got the idea of volunteering with other kids?"

"Maybe." Liam shrugged. "I never felt like I reached him. Stuart was no help, never wanted to talk about his son. His solution to their widening estrangement was to gift Ollie with bigger and better things."

That pattern held true. Ava heard through her sister's gossip grapevine that young Oliver inherited a small fortune in property owned by Stuart. Though his mother was supposed to oversee these things until he turned twenty-one in a few years, Oliver already had access. "He has the boat, you know."

"Which boat?"

"The one Stuart wanted Deep Dive to add to the fleet. Apparently, he'd already purchased it. Now it belongs to Ollie."

Liam clarified. "The boat where Stuart died. The one he bought with money borrowed from Tancredo."

"Pay attention, sailor. We already figured out that Stuart bought the boat. Now we know it went to Ollie. He is the proud owner of a seven-year-old cabin cruiser with dual outboard motors, and I'm guessing he'll bring it to this dock because he specifically asked me to meet him here."

"Why use that boat?" Unreadable emotions flickered in his eyes. Sorrow? Melancholy? "Is it some kind of revenge because he hated Stuart? No, that can't be. When he was younger, Ollie worshipped his dad."

The father and son looked very much alike. When Ollie smiled—which wasn't often—he had Stuart's double dimples. Ava had noticed the resemblance at the funeral. Everybody in Narcissus had attended, and the mood couldn't have been more fraught. Holly shed copious tears as did several other women who claimed to be his one true love although none of them wore his wedding ring like Holly. The rest of the Whitcomb family held their tempers in check, remaining cool and aloof. No tears. No wailing. Not even from Oliver who spend most of the day staring at the toes of his Top-Siders and mumbling.

"I'm not sure what Ollie wants." She turned away from Liam; being close was too tempting. "He sounded angry on the phone. Angry and hurt."

"His aunt Serena paid off Fish to testify for the prosecution. She wants me in jail."

"How did you change Fish's mind?"

"Money talks. My purse is bigger and, therefore, louder."

She strolled down to the water's edge, moving away from Liam. He seemed calm and casual, unconcerned about the approaching danger. She stalked back toward him, entering the shadow to warn him. "Don't underestimate Ollie. He's seventeen, almost an adult."

"Capable of grown-up violence."

"And he's not coming to the lighthouse to see me. He's after you." She jabbed her forefinger into his chest to get his attention. Ollie had something he wanted to find out or wanted to say to the man who had been his father's partner and, for a time, his best friend. Though it might be appealing for Liam to talk with the teenager, Ollie was unpredictable and possibly hostile. "You can't trust him."

"At heart, he's a good kid."

"If you're wrong, you could end up in jail." She didn't want to cast doubts without evidence, but she had to convince him, to remind him of the danger. "Please, Liam, be smart. Stay hidden."

"I will." He caught her hand and raised it to his lips, brushing a light kiss across her knuckles. "I promise."

Though she appreciated the gesture, now wasn't the time for romance. She reclaimed her hand and gave him a no-nonsense scowl. "Leave your earbuds in so I can tell you when the coast is clear and you can return to the lighthouse. Until then, I'll be out of touch."

"I'll miss you."

She'd expected him to object and insist on overhearing her conversation with Ollie, but he made no such demands. Instead, he waved to her and stepped back into the deepest shadows behind the rocks. What was going on with him? Did he have some kind of plot in mind?

Overhead, the gulls and cormorants swooped through the haze that rolled across the sky and dimmed the midmorning sunlight. She concentrated on her breathing, which eased her anxiety as she slowly walked by the edge of the surf. At the far end of the beach, the cliffs receded into offshore rock formations that stood like sentries to guard this small cove.

When she first took up residence at the lighthouse, she felt secluded and protected from the rest of the world. Now she sensed an ominous threat coming closer and closer. The sea breeze carried dark secrets. The forest hid an ever-present danger. Not only was she worried about Liam, but she feared the unnamed murderer among them. Someone she'd met. A voice she'd heard. The phone in the back pocket of her cargo pants played a sea shanty ringtone. Caller ID read: Sis.

"Hey, Rachel. What's up?"

"What's up with you, babycakes? Already this morning, I've had three customers ask about you and your professor."

Aha! A chance to discover who was spreading gossip. "Was one of them Holly?"

"Matter of fact, yes. Holly and Serena Whitcomb and Hannah, the bartender at Mack's Lumberjack Tavern."

"What are they saying?"

"Holly always liked Liam, and she'll do anything to help. Serena blames him for her brother's death and wants to see him in jail. And Hannah…well, she has the hots for him." Rachel paused for a moment. "Holly agrees."

"Do me a favor," Ava said. "Ask her why she's still wearing her wedding and engagement rings."

Ava heard her sister pose the question. The next voice on the phone was Holly herself. "Stuart showed up on my doorstep and ordered me to sell the rings and split the cash with him. Can you believe that jerk? These rings are worth nearly a hundred thousand buckeroos. As if I'd share it with him. Hah! Being married to Stuart for sixteen years, I earned this jewelry."

"And you stuck the rings on your finger."

"I swore I'd never take them off. Since he's dead, I guess it's different. But I still like the idea of having a fortune at my fingertips." She gave an odd little giggle. "Oh well, nice talking to you, Ava. Here's your sister."

Rachel said, "I have another question for you, baby sis. Why did you invite Michael to stay with you at the lighthouse? Do you need him for protection?"

"Just for the sake of argument, what would you say if I told you I believed Liam was innocent and I'm investigating?"

"No, no, no, no you aren't. You're supposed to be the smart one in the family. How could you do something so silly?" Her volume went up. "Ava, the man is a fugitive. Stay away from him. If you help him, you're abetting."

"What if he's innocent?"

"That means somebody else is a killer," Rachel said logically. "They might come after you."

Not a pleasant thought. "Talk to you later, Rachel. Got to run."

While Ava watched, a sleek yacht with a dark red hull and a covered helm and cabin cruised into view and aimed toward the dock. Ollie had arrived.

Chapter Seventeen

Liam had questions for Ollie. The kid didn't owe him answers, but they'd been close at one time. Was he willing to play for Team Liam?

Hiding in the shadows under the cliff, he clenched his jaw and held himself back as he watched Ava and Ollie walk across the sand toward the path. The young man stood over six feet tall and moved with long, fast strides that caused Ava to trot in an effort to keep up with him. *Inconsiderate. And sloppy.* His baggy board shorts hung low on his skinny hips, and his faded Kurt Cobain T-shirt looked like grunge and probably smelled like teen spirit. How had this sullen punk emerged from the cute kid who dressed as a starfish for Halloween? A waterproof backpack hung from his shoulders—a reminder that Ollie told Ava he had something important to share. The pack wasn't big enough to hold a club or an oar or whatever was used as a murder weapon, but there was plenty of room for the drugs that were used to knock Liam unconscious.

Though he hoped the kid wasn't guilty of anything more sinister than being a teenager, he was suspicious. He hadn't spent the past couple of days hiding in a secret passageway, crammed into the trunk of a Hyundai and peeking down from the top of a lighthouse for nothing. Ava had advised him to stay unseen, and she was right. His real goal could be accomplished without speaking to Ollie or anybody else. Liam needed to find the truth.

His psychologist suggested that he might arouse more of his buried memories by placing himself close to the situation where the trauma occurred. And there sat the yacht where Stuart was killed—a floating crime scene. The cabin cruiser had a midsize cabin with the helm at the front. The galley, fridge, benches and table were tucked neatly under the hardtop. Additional space at the stern—between the covered cabin and the twin Yamaha F300 outboard motors— provided storage and more seating in case they happened to find a couple of women in tiny bikinis who wanted a ride.

The yacht hadn't been outfitted as a salvage vessel. For the purposes of Deep Dive, it was too small and too pretty. When Stuart welcomed him aboard this craft, named *The Reckless* by the previous owner, Liam immediately told him that the boat didn't suit their business. Yes, a cylindrical rack could be added for scuba gear and oxygen, but salvage work could be messy. Clearly, this cruiser hadn't been designed for that. This was a pickup yacht with a queen-size bed under the hull and a well-stocked bar in the galley. Liam had a fairly good idea why his partner wanted *The Reckless*. Good for Stuart, but not for him. There hadn't been a woman in his life before Ava, and she probably wouldn't be enchanted by this fancy-ass cabin cruiser.

He stepped out from the shadow and approached the dock where the boat was moored. While guiding the twin engine yacht through open water, Ollie had managed nicely. Stuart made sure his son had taken the required boating safety classes and received certification. No doubt, the teenager would make good use of this beautiful boat.

From the dock, Liam stepped onto the dive platform beside the rear-mounted motors and entered the outdoor seating area with gleaming white benches and long, waterproof cushions with dark red, beige and white stripes. The top of each bench opened to reveal more storage. Liam took a look inside, hoping he might find a wet suit and scuba gear. No such luck. He saw life jackets, water guns, a couple of boogie boards, hoodie sweatshirts and other teenager gear.

When he'd been on board with Stuart before the murder, the lighting had been different. On that cloudless, bright day, they cruised away from Newport in the early afternoon. Liam remembered the warmth of sunshine on his face and the top of his head.

Today, hazy clouds blanketed the skies, and the wind was a whisper. On the moored yacht, he went through the covered cabin to the helm where a captain's chair faced the wheel and the cherrywood dash which was equipped with the usual dials and switches, including a GPS navigation system and VHF radio. When he'd been with Stuart, he'd commented on the cleanliness and elegance of *The Reckless*. "But we don't need a luxury yacht in our fleet."

"You've got to think big," Stuart had said as he sailed away from the marina and headed for the open sea. "Suppose we're entertaining a wealthy, important client, and we need to show him that we're worthy of handling his business."

"It'll take more than polished cherrywood trim to impress." This clash had been consistent between the partners. Stuart had been far more ambitious, constantly seeking lucrative deals, while Liam dedicated himself to research and old shipwrecks. "We have as much business as we can handle."

"Think bigger." He had gestured grandly to the galley behind the helm. "Help yourself to food and beer."

"No champagne?"

"Sorry, partner. I'm not going to waste bubbly on you."

Liam stared through the windshield at the massive, offshore rock where gulls and cormorants and murres nested. His last hours with Stuart weren't the makings of epic memories. *Same old, same old.* Their relationship had been tarnished by years of squabbling and fussing and undertaking inane projects and purchases. Like *The Reckless.* Liam had already spoken to the psychologist about this minor argument with his partner. Then, he'd described, in excruciating detail, the way he'd put together his lunch, consisting of a soggy, premade tuna salad sandwich, guacamole and chips. Also, a longneck handcrafted beer.

The therapist had pointed out that the tuna salad or the guac could have been dosed with any of the many "date rape" drugs that worked their way quickly through the system and wouldn't have shown up in the toxicology screen that took place hours after ingesting. Though appalled by how easy it was to knock someone out, Liam believed he'd been drugged. How else could he explain the woozy feeling that had overwhelmed him? The yacht had cruised farther from shore until they were surrounded by the rolling waves of the Pacific. The rhythm lulled him. His eyelids grew heavy.

Stuart had left the helm and joined him in the stern lounging area where they both sprawled across the cushions and nursed their beers. Had Stuart been eating anything? He didn't recall. The twin Yamaha motors were silent, and Liam had heard the waves lap against the side of the yacht. No other vessels had been in sight, and they'd drifted miles away from shore. He'd felt peaceful and relaxed.

His memories before he passed out had already been recalled, including his recent flash of the inflatable boat that had approached *The Reckless* and the argument between two men when Stuart said he'd changed his mind. On the day of the murder, Liam fell into an unconscious state, his mind went blank and he remembered nothing until he awoke and found Stuart's body. Bleeding from a head wound, he was unconscious and near death.

Hoping to fill in the blank space, Liam arranged himself against the cushions, imitating his position on the day of the murder. He closed his eyes and opened his mind to memory. The taste of avocado, the crunch of chips and the cool slide of beer down his gullet. What had Stuart said to him? Something about management and how the yacht would be an advantage when selling their services. "Besides," Stuart had said, "we deserve some luxury. We ought to be able to have some fun."

"Do you need money?" Liam remembered himself asking.

"Hell, no. I'm richer than you'll ever be."

"Then…why?" His voice had been weak. His words slurred. He'd only had one beer, not enough to be intoxicated. What was wrong with him? "Why do you want Deep Dive to buy this boat? Tax write-off?"

"Relax, buddy. You worry too much. Not important. It's only business."

Only business. That was Stuart's justification for everything.

Sitting in the boat at the dock, Liam's mind went blank, just as it had when he was at sea with Stuart. But now, he could take control. He kept his eyes closed, regulated his breathing and waited for his indistinct memories to take solid form. His thoughts were uncensored, fanciful. He imagined a mermaid leaping through the waves with her long, chestnut brown hair streaming behind her. She had Ava's eyes and her full lips. He heard the musical sound of her laughter. *A siren song.* This beautiful reverie was interrupted by the chug of a motor from the inflatable boat that docked at the rear of the cabin cruiser.

Someone else had joined them on the yacht. But who? Was this a planned rendezvous or a happenstance meeting?

Must have been planned. They were in the middle of no-where. Someone had come looking for them.

Stuart's voice echoed inside his skull. *I changed my mind.* Was this a deal gone wrong? Liam struggled to hear more. The other voice—indistinguishable, garbled and loud—had argued, had told Stuart they had to do it his way. Their dis-agreement had grown more and more heated.

Liam remembered his need to respond. Instinctively, he'd wanted to defend his partner. Trying to reach out, his arm had fallen limply onto his lap. His legs splayed. He couldn't move. His head felt like it weighed a hundred pounds. His neck was too weak to support it. His tongue lolled. His mouth tasted like cotton.

The argument had expanded, louder than the surf and the cries of sea birds. A ferocious, roaring noise. *Help Stuart.* He had to help Stuart.

With a huge effort, Liam forced his eyelids to open. He squinted toward the covered cabin and saw the fight turn physical. A male figure in a black wet suit raised a heavy-duty, aluminum oar and swung it like a baseball bat. He hit Stuart at the back of his skull, then again and again.

Liam jolted awake, left the vivid memory behind as he jumped to his feet on the stern deck. The horror of his friend's death and his inability to stop the killer chilled him to the core. And yet, he felt a deep, abiding sense of relief. He spoke aloud, reassuring himself. "It wasn't me. I didn't kill him."

He had witnessed the attack on Stuart. Didn't know the identity of the murderer but had uncovered additional evi-dence. The man in the wet suit had approached on an inflatable with an outboard motor, similar to a Zodiac. Unfortunately, that fact didn't narrow the field. Many people at the marina had inflatable boats. *Deep Dive* owned two.

Concentrating hard, Liam tried to identify the man who

attacked Stuart. They seemed to be nearly the same height and average build. In the wet suit, it was hard to notice his body type, and Liam hadn't seen his face. He seemed to have a business relationship with Stuart, which pointed toward Quincy or Tancredo.

He heard a voice in his ear. Ava spoke through the mic. Not a mermaid's song but a slightly panicked warning. "Jess-hole is here. He's already on the path, coming down to the beach. You've got to hide."

There wasn't time to leap off the boat onto the dock and run across the open beach to the shadows under the cliff. Liam went to the helm and opened the hatch leading to the bedroom under the bow. Not an ideal hiding place but it would have to do. Hoping Ava had her earbuds in, he said, "I'm in the bedroom under the bow on *The Reckless*."

AVA COULDN'T BELIEVE what she'd just heard through her earbuds. Why in the world had Liam gone onto the boat? What did he think he was going to prove? She came to a halt on the beach at the end of the path and called out to Jessop, who charged across the sand ahead of her, ignoring the friendly yapping from sea lions. "Deputy, please, wait for me."

He swiveled around. His pointy nose aimed in her direction. "Don't tell me what to do."

Desperate for an excuse to stop him, she blurted, "Search warrant."

"Doesn't work that way. You can demand a warrant before letting me into your house, but this is a public beach. I don't need your permission to search for the fugitive."

Ollie stepped up behind her. "But you don't have my okay to board my boat."

Jess-hole's eyes narrowed to slits. "I can't believe some

damn kid is giving me orders. The both of you can go straight to hell."

She heard the heavy clomping from her brother descending the path and kicking rocks out of his way. On the beach, Michael strode past her, nodded to the sea lions and went directly toward the deputy who rested his hand on the butt of his holstered pistol. In a deep voice, calm and yet somehow threatening, he said, "I strongly advise you not to swear at my sister."

"You don't scare me, Donovan. You're an ex-con. I can take you into custody."

"What's the charge?"

"Harboring a fugitive."

"You've got no proof."

Ava heard others joining them. Her responsible brother, Jerome, who had never been in trouble with the authorities, and Fish Finley climbed down the hill and charged across the beach to stand on either side of Michael. They made a formidable trio. Michael looked like an archetypal cowboy who could easily wrestle a 650-pound steer to the ground. After years of working construction, Jerome was muscular and tanned, wearing a hard hat. Fish, a shorter man, exuded a wiry strength under the black leather biker jacket he wore to lunch. Ava smiled to herself. All they needed was a chief with a feather headdress to be the Village People.

"Well, Deputy, I hope you brought a bus," Jerome said. "If you arrest Michael, you'd better arrest all of us."

"Me, too," Ollie chirped as he joined them.

Bursting with pride, Ava inserted herself as the peacemaker. "We all have a busy day ahead of us. If you're done here, Deputy, we'd like to get back to work."

Jess-hole cast an angry glance toward the yacht moored at the dock. He wanted to board, wanted to search. And if he found what he was looking for... A shudder twitched across her shoulders. In spite of their bravado and support, Liam was still in danger. The deputy could come back here with others and force the issue. They could tear the place apart until they found him.

For the moment, they were safe. She decided to take the win as Jessop retreated toward the path. The other men followed, and she stopped Ollie. Quietly, she asked, "Do you mind if I board your yacht? There's something I need to look for."

"No problem." He almost smiled. His cheeks flushed. "I'm on your side."

"Tell the guys I'll be up there in a minute."

Running across the sand toward the dock, anger churned in her gut. She didn't like being rescued by her big brothers and hated being threatened by Jess-hole. In addition, Liam's irresponsible actions really ticked her off. If Jessop had found him, all their efforts would have been overturned. They all could have been arrested. Why didn't he just stay hidden? Glancing over her shoulder to make sure Jessop wasn't watching, she stepped onto the stern deck beside the motors and scampered to the helm where she tapped on the hatch beside the wheel.

Forgetting she wore the mic and he could hear her every word, she shouted, "Liam, let me in."

He whipped open the door, grasped her arm and pulled her into the dimly lit bedroom under the bow. She stumbled. In a swift, smooth move, he used her forward momentum to guide her onto the queen-size bed with a dark blue quilt.

"Angry?" he asked.

Flat on her back, she glared up at him. The hazy sunlight through a small porthole shone on his huge, incandescent smile. "What's so funny?"

"Not a joke," he said. "It's truth. And it's good, really good. Ready?"

"Just tell me."

"I didn't kill Stuart."

Not exactly a big reveal. She knew he had doubts about his innocence, but she hadn't for a minute believed that he was capable of murder. No matter what form his amnesia took, he surely would have recalled a lethal outburst. "Well, of course you didn't."

"I wasn't sure." Lying on his side with his head propped on his fist, he reached with the other hand and caressed her cheek. "I've never actually blacked out before, but I've come close. And Stuart knew me well, maybe better than anybody else. He knew how to push my buttons."

"You cared about him."

His voice softened. "I miss him, Ava. I never mourned my friend."

Clearly, Liam had undergone a transformation, but she wasn't sure how or why. "What changed?"

"I remembered." He rolled onto his back beside her and stared at the low ceiling. "My psychologist suggested that I put myself into situations similar to the murder, close my eyes, try to meditate—which is something I don't do very well—and let my mind wander."

"What did you see?"

"A guy in a black wet suit clubbed Stuart with an oar. I wanted to help but I couldn't move. Felt like my arms and legs were weighted down. Then I passed out again."

"But you saw the killer?"

"Right."

"Don't keep me in suspense." She shifted position so that she was hovering over him. "Who was it?"

"I don't know. Didn't see his face. In the wet suit, he looked average height and build. Nothing unusual about him."

"You are the most infuriating man I've ever known." She climbed on top of him, straddled his hips and planted her fists on either side of his head on the pillow. "You have to stop taking risks. Get off this boat. Go back to the lighthouse tower. Tonight, we can figure out what we should do next."

"Doesn't matter. I can turn myself in to Woodburn right now."

"What?"

"I didn't commit murder. The truth will come out."

She didn't think of herself as a cynic, but life had taught her that good didn't always triumph. Michael had spent several years in prison for a crime he hadn't committed. "I don't want to pop your happiness balloon, but—"

"Let me have this moment."

He flipped over on top of her and held her down while he kissed her. Unwilling to release her righteous rage, she struggled. The friction of their bodies rubbing together drove coherent thought from her mind. He was strong, dominating. As an avowed feminist, she shouldn't like it. But she did. Her anger turned too quickly to passion. His tongue did amazing things inside her mouth, and his hands skimmed across her body, touching one erogenous zone after another. She wished she could abandon herself to these feelings.

Not now. Ollie could come back to the boat at any moment. They could be discovered. Liam could be arrested.

She shoved him off her. "No, and I mean it."

"Later?"

"Not making any promises." She straightened her windbreaker as she climbed off the bed and pressed her back against the paneled wall beside the porthole. "I'll let you know when it's safe to go back to the lighthouse. In the meantime, get off the boat."

"Bossy."

"You bet I am."

"Do you know the best thing about knowing for sure that I'm not a murderer?"

After that incredible kiss, she doubted he was about to go high-minded and moralistic on her. "What?

"You," he said. "I don't have to feel guilty about my attraction to you. There's no barrier between us. I don't have to hold back. The truth set us free."

"I'm not following your reasoning."

"All along, I've been telling you that you deserve better. Bad boys, con artists and cheats aren't good enough for you, Ava. As a man accused of murder, I had to accept that I had no right to approach you. But now…"

He left the words dangling, and she completed the thought. "You think you deserve me because you're not a cold-blooded killer."

A goofy grin spread across his face. "Sounds weird to say it that way, but yeah."

"You're not setting the bar real high, are you?"

He grasped her arm again and gave her a hard, quick kiss. "And you deserve me."

"Lucky me." She dug into the large side pocket of her windbreaker and pulled out a small, leather-bound volume. "As if your ego needed any more boosting, you'll be happy to know that Ollie remembered the time you spent together. He even smiled when he talked about your fishing trips. And he left you a present. A daily captain's log from Stuart."

"I'll be damned," Liam mumbled. "I should have thought of that sooner. He was always writing lists and keeping logs. This could be the evidence we need.

"Exactly." She tossed the book onto the bed. "It ought to make for interesting reading."

Chapter Eighteen

After a morning spent hiding among the rocks under the cliff and sneaking into the forest when Jess-hole returned with two other deputies and a search warrant, Liam had watched *The Reckless* cruise away from the dock. He'd wanted to thank Ollie for believing in him. The kid had really come through, and Stuart's captain log might provide the evidence they needed.

In the early afternoon, he got the all clear from Ava through his earbuds. Though tempted to hop onto Fish's motorboat that was parked at the small dock under the overhanging cliff, he retreated to his hideout in the lighthouse tower. Stretched out on his belly on the sleeping bag, he unfastened the thick rubber band holding the book closed and gave his full attention to the pages in the dark blue, pocket-size volume with a gold anchor emblazoned on the cover. On the first page, written in Stuart's elegant script was the date—January 1 of this year—and the words: *Captain's Log.*

Liam flipped through the unlined pages, which had no particular rhyme or reason for the lapses between dates. Sometimes, there were three entries on consecutive days. Sometimes, ten days passed between notes. Only about twenty pages had been used from January until the middle of March, the day before Stuart died. On each recorded page, he had written the date, location, temperature and a sentence or two about the day's business. On some pages, there was only a name—usually a woman, a place and a time. No need to explain the purpose of these meetings with the ladies. Nonetheless, Liam would pass on these references to Willis, his private investigator. One or more of Stuart's girl-friends might provide a lead.

Carefully, Liam turned the pages and read, remembering the tail end of his nearly twenty-year friendship with Stuart. On January 8 at their first yearly meeting to discuss plans for Deep Dive, they had argued. Loudly. That might have been the day when Fish overheard him threaten Stuart with bodily harm. Stuart's note for that day: "LB is a bilge rat. If I had the $, I would buy that sucker out."

LB had to stand for Liam Brody. He smiled as he ran his fingers across the perfect cursive writing, which Stuart told him resulted from years in a private academy practicing pen-manship. The term "bilge rat" instead of something more obscene also came from early training. Stuart seldom swore. Though definitely a manly man, he'd been excessively tidy. As personality disorders went, OCD wasn't a bad one. Liam had taken advantage of his partner's need for order and left all the cataloging of salvage items and artifacts to him—a decision that might have come back to bite him on the bum.

He reread the final entry: "Must repay the loan. Tomor-row, I must convince LB to join my clandestine op or to sell me his shares."

Finally, Liam had the real reason why Stuart had taken him into the middle of the ocean on his new cabin cruiser. But the entry didn't mention drugging him. If Liam hadn't agreed to participate in the "clandestine" operation—which had to involve smuggling objects they recovered as salvage—and had also refused to sell, what was Stuart's game plan?

Liam got off the sleeping bag and went to the lighthouse windows. Though the glass hadn't been cleaned in years, he still had a spectacular view of the endless Pacific horizon. Leaving Stuart in charge of their inventory had been a mistake. Faced with treasures that had been lost for years, the temptation had been too great. Most of the objects they recovered weren't worth much, but some were valuable. And they were right there for the taking. If Stuart didn't record the piece in his ledger, there was no evidence that it existed. He was able to smuggle whatever he wanted with a low probability of being discovered.

Standing at the window at the verge of the cliff, Liam continued to study the captain's log. Using an old-fashioned pen-and-paper notebook instead of writing on a digital tablet or computer suited Stuart's compulsive nature. Many times, Liam had found him with pen in hand as he worked on lists and entries. After he recorded the bits and pieces of salvage, he gave his lists to an office worker, someone like Maxine Gallo, to put into a computer file.

Dammit, Stuart, what were you thinking? For the first time since he'd found the body, Liam felt the sting of regret. He'd never have the chance to set things right with his partner. Never again would the two of them argue. They'd never stand on deck watching a western sunset while sharing a fine Pinot Noir. Or go clamming. Or fishing. *I miss him.*

The investigation took on a new purpose. Solving Stuart's murder meant saving Liam from wrongful accusation, and it also meant justice for his partner who might have been annoying as hell but didn't deserve to die.

He reread the January 8 entry. Why did Stuart comment that he didn't have enough money to buy out Liam's shares? The Whitcomb family had major wealth and lots of property. Stuart often bragged about his riches. Liam never doubted him, but the minute he'd mentioned smuggling to his lawyers and the private eye, they dug into Stuart's bank accounts and investments. He appeared to be solid.

Other evidence indicated Stuart wasn't as fiscally sound as he'd once been. Rather than arranging for a rendezvous at the luxurious Heathman Hotel in Portland, he'd opted to take his date to a cheesy little motel on the beach. Holly's engagement and wedding ring were another example. She'd told Ava that he demanded she sell the rings and split the cash with him. Holly said he sounded desperate which was why she refused to cooperate and kept her jewelry for revenge, flashing those diamonds every chance she got.

On the other hand, Stuart had recently acquired *The Reckless*, an expensive cabin cruiser. How had he paid for it? More than likely, he'd used the money he borrowed from Tancredo. Was it some kind of trade or a deal worked out with the people who were fencing salvage for him? Liam's private eye had informed him that Stuart's records were clean and showed no apparent association with smuggling or fencing operations. *Nice work, Willis.* The PI had stayed on the job and kept in touch with bits of info. Maxine Gallo could be the source of more details about his finances. Had Willis made contact with her?

Liam activated his laptop using the portable charger, intending to type another email to Willis about Maxine. Might be a waste of time. How could that salty old dame know more about Stuart's finances than his lawyers, the prosecuting attorney and other law enforcement investigators? It was possible, totally possible. Over the years, Liam had learned that sometimes the least likely people had the most information.

A new email from Willis gave him a fresh burst of hope. The PI had tracked down a fence in Portland who did business with Quincy over the years and had receipts and records showing salvage that had been recovered by Deep Dive. Proof! Liam's suspicions were confirmed. He responded to Willis, telling him to inform his attorney of the evidence. *Thank god, his computer and electronics were encoded and couldn't be traced because he was leaving a wide trail.*

An immediate return email gave an address and phone number for Maxine Gallo in Nye Beach where she had a storefront shop selling ceramics and hanging macramé holders. Name of her shop: Knots and Pots. According to Willis, Maxine refused to talk to anybody but Liam, preferably in person.

Did he dare to take that risk?

His knee-jerk reaction told him to go to Nye Beach and pursue the investigation on his own. Law enforcement had bungled the case. As soon as they decided he was the killer, they didn't bother to dig deeper. *Not true for all of them.* Marshal Woodburn had shown himself to be competent and critical of the investigation. Might be smart to hand Stuart's captain log over to him and let the professional detectives follow up on these leads as well as following up with the fence in Portland. But his gut told him that Maxine had more information about Stuart. She knew his secrets. Liam needed to see her.

He sent another email to Willis, along with the promise of a sizable bonus for his outstanding investigative work. Three words summed up his plan: *I'll visit Maxine.*

Before he left the relative safety of the lighthouse, Liam wanted to read the entire log and glean whatever evidence he could. There were several notations of meetings with PQ, Peter Quincy, and CT, Charlie Tancredo. Apparently, Stuart quarreled with them as often as he fought with Liam. His problem with Tancredo revolved around impossible demands from people he called "the Canadians" who might be part of a north-based drug cartel.

"Damn it, Stuart," he muttered. "Why would you get involved with drugs?"

The interactions with Quincy seemed less dire and more profitable. Not that fencing stolen salvage and cargo wasn't criminal fraud. Such transactions violated maritime laws and restrictions. If they'd been found out, Deep Dive would have lost everything from swim fins to sonar equipment.

Liam stared at the pages in the captain's log, trying to make sense of Stuart's deeds and motivations. His thoughts ping-ponged between anger at Stuart and confusion about why he'd gotten involved with smugglers and fences—people who were clearly not the type of companion usually associated with the eldest son of the Whitcomb dynasty.

The entry on February 2 said: "CT promises we'll have no trouble from the law. They leave us alone. We pay them well." No doubt, crooked officials could be bribed to ignore a minor smuggling operation. Deputy Jessop came to mind. He'd be the first in line with his hand out.

But Liam had become well-acquainted with law enforcement over the past weeks, and he didn't believe they were all corrupt. Not to mention that the U. S. Coast Guard would be part of an investigation into international smuggling and possibly the FBI. For some unknown reason, Tancredo thought they had immunity. And he'd given Stuart a substantial loan. Why? To what purpose?

Trust no one. Suspect everyone.

Right now, Liam's best alternative seemed simple: *Keep investigating.*

Maxine Gallo awaited him in Nye Beach, only twenty miles away by motorboat. Though he doubted she'd turn him over to the law, visiting her shop represented a huge risk. Nye Beach—a combination of quaint shops and seaside condos—nestled in the historic part of Newport. People in that area knew him. But he couldn't stay away. Maxine might be able to provide the last piece of evidence to exonerate him. He hoped she could shed light on Stuart's false inventory records. Or she might be able to explain how he physically removed the objects from the dive boat, where he kept them and how he transported them to the end destination.

Quincy had to be involved in that process. And maybe Tancredo. The harbormaster might have been on board the dive boat while working on a "clandestine" job with Stuart and Quincy.

After Liam talked to Maxine, he figured it was time to contact his attorney and turn himself in to the police. With the captain's log, testimony from the Portland fence, indications of fraudulent inventory records regarding salvage and—last but not least—potential narcotraffic from Canada, his investigation raised questions about Stuart's murder. The police inquiry would need to be re-opened. Liam knew he'd be in trouble for violating bail, but that was nothing compared to murder changes.

He stood at the smudged window at the top of the lighthouse, looked out to sea and considered. *Should he voluntarily surrender to the police?* Thus far, he'd been lucky. He hadn't been discovered, and Ava hadn't been charged with aiding and abetting.

Second thoughts rose up like a tidal wave. Why risk the trip to Nye Beach? *Why not turn himself in right now?* Within an hour, he could be back in custody and on his way to jail where he'd wait until the charges against him were dismissed. His high-priced attorney was on speed dial. All it took to end his fugitive peril was the touch of a button.

He wasn't ready give up. Liam had a deeply compelling reason to see Maxine and wait until morning to contact his attorney. That reason had a name: Ava Donovan.

He didn't want to leave with unspoken words hanging between them. There could be no misunderstanding. His connection with her went deeper than any danger he might experience, deeper than the threat of prison. His mind filled with images of Ava. Running across the beach past the sea lions and the gulls. In the kitchen of the cottage wearing flannel pajamas. Hiding with him in the secret passage. He grinned as he remembered her ascent to the top of the lighthouse wearing her crazy, red, platform sandals. The glow of sunset colored her cheeks as she stood on the widow's walk.

The shape of her face was perfection. Her primrose blue eye shone with a gentleness that reflected her compassionate self. Her lips were made for whispering into his ear. Didn't matter what she said, every word soothed him and aroused him.

Tonight, he would fulfill the desire that had been building inside him since he first saw her. He couldn't wait to gather her sweet, slender body in his embrace, to run his hands over her smooth skin and tangle his fingers in her curly hair.

Though he never would have asked to be charged with murder and driven to Ava for help, he was glad about the way things had turned out. She'd changed him. In a few short days, she'd given his life meaning and made him a better man. Tonight, he'd show her how grateful he was to have her back in his life. And he wouldn't let her leave him again.

He gazed beyond the rock where the gulls, cormorants and murres nested to the rolling Pacific waves. The sea was relatively calm, waiting for him and for Ava. Below the edge of the overhanging cliff, the dock was hidden. Fish's motorboat was moored and ready.

Liam stepped into the sunlight prepared to wrap up this investigation. Tonight would be his reward.

Chapter Nineteen

Heading north along the coast, Ava sat beside Liam in Fish's turquoise blue, nineteen-foot-long fishing boat that was clean with equipment neatly stowed but still smelled of fish. Though the outboard motor maintained a steady pace though calm seas with winds of only five to ten knots, the chill Pacific frothed around them as Liam guided the small craft toward Nye Beach. The ocean breeze brought ruddy color to his sharp cheekbones and the stubborn jut of his jaw. His steely gaze studied the swells of the waves as they rode past forestland, rocky shores and seaside towns.

She harkened back to the time when they'd first met six years ago, and he'd directed his maritime class on a salvage expedition. Whether steering a humble fishing boat or captaining his dive ship, her former professor was more comfortable on the sea than the land, but she couldn't help wondering if they were sailing into disaster.

She tossed her head and leaned into the rush of wind through her hair. "Tell me again, Mr. Fugitive. What are you going to do if approached by an officer of the law?"

"Surrender peacefully. I'm ready to turn myself in." He snugged an arm around her waist, pulled her close and planted a swift kiss on her mouth. "Don't think about what might happen, Ava. Concentrate on this moment. This is where we're supposed to be, you and me. It feels right, so damn right. Have I ever mentioned how much you remind me of a mermaid?"

Not a fantasy that appealed to her. Ava liked having legs. "What changed? Why aren't you hiding anymore?"

"With Stuart's captain's log, the testimony of the fence in Portland and my returning memories, my attorney has enough new evidence to demand further investigation. The trial will have to be postponed, maybe indefinitely."

She understood his reasoning, but he'd left much unsaid. "With all that new information, do we really need to take this trip to Nye Beach to meet with your former assistant?"

"Maxine Gallo worked more with Stuart than with me. She might be able to shed light on his fake inventory lists. Also, she hinted that she might have more information."

"Couldn't you just call her?"

"I trust Maxine, but I'll know more if I talk to her face-to-face."

She understood what he meant. Body language and facial expression were invaluable indicators. She'd known from the moment she saw him that Liam wasn't a murderer. As if she'd recognize a killer when she saw one. "How can you spot a lie?"

"I'm told the nose grows really long."

"Cute." She groaned. "And how do you tell the good guys from the villains?"

"The good ones don't come at you with knives drawn."

"Here's something I've never understood," she said. "I have a friend who can tell at a glance if a guy is wealthy or broke, no matter what he's wearing or what he says."

"You've got to look deep into his eyes. The rich dudes have dollar signs."

"But you don't."

"Maybe I'm not as rich as you think."

More likely, wealth didn't matter to him. Liam didn't run his life based on his bank account which was why Stuart could swindle him. She continued their game. "What do you see in a murderer's eyes?"

"A tiny skull and crossbones." He grinned. "Now I've got a question for you. Look into my eyes and tell me what's there."

She twisted around so she could see his face while he continued to monitor their forward progress through the waves. Golden rays of sunlight spilled over him. The glow reflected in his sexy gray eyes. Instead of a skull and crossbones, she could have sworn that she saw a radiant valentine. "A heart."

"Really? I hoped there would be something X-rated."

"You're so naughty."

"Guilty."

While his sea captain's gaze stayed fixed to the course ahead of them, his grasp of her tightened. The hand at her waist stroked upward over her rib cage until he cupped her breast. Her back arched as she leaned toward him, wanting more. His thumb flicked her taut nipple, and she gave a gasp of surprise and delight.

Step by step, inch by inch the walls of restraint erected between them began to crumble. He was a good man, not a murderer. Liam would fit perfectly with her loud, loving family. With no more need to hold back, she was free to enjoy these amazing sensations she'd fantasized about for years.

Though she wanted to ignore the dark cloud on their horizon, she had to face the shadow. When he turned himself in, he'd be taken into custody. She wouldn't be able to see him or talk to him. After these days of being intensely connected, his absence would leave a terrible void in her life. "I don't want you to go."

"It won't be for long. I'm coming back for you, Ava. We've

been given a second chance, and I don't intend to waste it. And tonight…" He kissed her again. "Tonight is for us."

She snuggled against his chest. The warmth radiating from his body lit a fire inside her. She felt cozy and sexy at the same time, and she prayed he wouldn't be arrested on the sidewalks of the little seaside town before nightfall. "First, I should take care of business."

"By all means."

"I ought to call Peter Quincy and tell him that I'm not going to go with him tomorrow to see Tancredo."

"Good idea. Sever that connection. At best, Quincy and Tancredo are sea slugs. At worst, they're murderers."

Staying in Liam's embrace, she took out her phone and made the call. As expected, she got Quincy's answering machine. Speaking loudly so she'd be heard over the whir of the outboard motor, she canceled their meeting at Newport, giving no other reason than "something else came up."

When she ended the call, she frowned at the phone. "I hope Quincy's dirty deeds won't affect my relationship with Georgina. Do you really think he's the one who murdered Stuart?"

"Not sure," he said. "Stuart's last entry in his captain's log on the day before he was murdered said he planned to meet me and Quincy on the fancy new boat. The two of them wanted to convince me to sell my shares in Deep Dive to Stuart. He and Quincy would form a new salvage company. There was no mention of drugging or violence."

"Why did you pass out?"

"The way I figure, Quincy must have decided to take matters into his own hands. He laced my food with some kind of drug he got from Tancredo. Then he approached in his inflatable boat."

"You remembered the boat."

"But I don't know if it was Quincy or Tancredo who boarded *The Reckless*. Could have been both. I heard a loud argument. Didn't recognize the voice. In my last vision, I saw a man in a black wet suit whack Stuart with an oar."

"Quincy is known for having a hot temper," she said.

"Tancredo as well."

"Poor Georgina." She gazed toward shore as they passed the entrance to the Port of Newport where Liam's dive boat was docked and Tancredo was harbormaster. The arched bridge—part of Highway 101—spanned the entrance to Yaquina Bay. "She seems truly fond of Quincy. And he's attentive to her."

"Is there a name for a male gold digger?"

"I think it's a gender-neutral term." And she had something else to consider. "Georgina isn't going to be happy with me if I'm partly responsible for putting her husband in prison. I might be out of a job."

"I wouldn't worry about it." His busy hand at her waist slid lower, and he gave her bottom a gentle, affectionate pat. "Your boss wouldn't want to be married to a murderer."

He spoke with a confidence Ava didn't feel. Though Georgina was respectful of history and the environment, she came from a family of heartless lumber barons who were responsible for horrendous working conditions and vast deforestation. "The Solomon family wasn't exactly known for fair play and high moral standards."

"We don't know for sure that Quincy is the killer. There are unanswered questions about Tancredo. Why did he make that quarter-million-dollar loan to Stuart? He gave Stuart a task, but I don't know what it was. And there's the whole issue of drug smuggling. If Tancredo was involved with a northern cartel, he might have struck the fatal blow to preserve his criminal empire."

Ava preferred that scenario. She squeezed her eyes closed, trying to erase her casual thoughts of murder. How could she be so easygoing while thinking about the death of a person she knew? This wasn't a board game. There had been real blood. Real violence.

On a bluff jutting into the ocean, she spotted the Yaquina Head Lighthouse. She pointed toward the iconic silhouette. "One of the most photographed light towers on the Oregon coast. This used to be called Cape Foulweather. The lighthouse is ninety-three feet tall, almost twice as high as Cape Absolute."

"Did you do research there?"

"Frequently. Yaquina Head was decommissioned in the 1930s but has been carefully restored and is fully operational, still using the originally Fresnel lantern. The light doesn't revolve. Instead, there's a signature beam—on for two seconds, then off for two, then on for two and off for fourteen before starting the sequence again."

"You've done your homework."

"That's kind of my thing."

Thoughts of Elizabeth Mayes, the widow of Cape Absolute lighthouse, scrolled through her mind like an old-time movie. Similar to Stuart, Elizabeth had written of her activities, hopes, plans and regrets in her daily log. Maybe Ava should do the same. Keeping a journal while she did renovations on the lighthouse might be a good idea, especially if she decided to put together a book about the project.

Liam veered into a small inlet where the rough sea went smooth. Houses and condos perched on the cliff overlooking the water. "Fish gave me the name of a guy who owns a house in this cove. As it turns out, I know him, too. He doesn't mind if small boats moor at his dock for an hour or so."

"An hour? We're not going to be at Maxine's shop that long, are we? I promised Fish we'd return by six o'clock."

"Plenty of time," Liam said as he cut the motor, expertly guided the boat to a mooring place and hopped onto the pier. He took her hand to help her come ashore before he tied the bowline to the cleat. "We'll be back to the lighthouse a few hours before dark."

Her cell phone showed over two hours before they were due back which should be plenty of time. She made a quick call to Michael at the lightkeeper's cottage. Of course, he didn't answer. Though taking care of her older brother wasn't really her responsibility, Ava wanted to show her appreciation for his help and protection. She texted him a note about dinner. Probably they'd pick up a pizza. Even though her number one focus was spending time alone with Liam tonight, Ava never ever forgot her family and friends.

She picked her way along the narrow path at the foot of the cliff where coastal grasses, weeds and lupins sprouted among the craggy rocks. A rough wooden staircase with a handrail led to street level. Nye Beach represented a historic part of Newport where quaint, eclectic storefronts, coffee shops and specialty restaurants lined the sidewalks below two- and three-story apartments with views of the boardwalk and the beach. On a Monday in April, the long, wide swath of packed sand wasn't crowded. Dogs chased in and out of the water. Kids built castles and flew multicolor kites while their parents set up lawn chairs to watch the waves.

When Ava paused to take in the scene, Liam laced his fingers with hers and gave a squeeze as though they were a typical couple out for a stroll instead of a couple of law-breakers wanted by the police. His touch felt familiar and natural, giving her a pleasant sense of well-being. She gazed up at him. Three days' growth of stubble gave him a rugged look, but he didn't seem scruffy. He appeared to be relaxed, like a guy on vacation.

They mingled with tourists on the sidewalk and easily located Knots and Pots. The name of the shop was written in fancy, old-fashioned script, and the front window displayed several hanging planters in a literal rainbow of colors ranging from fire engine red to deep purple. When they stepped inside, a bell jangled loudly. A tall, broad-shouldered woman with wild, curly hair—also in rainbow shades—popped out from the rear of the shop. Hard to miss her; she dressed in stripes and paisley over tie-dyed leggings. Her handsome, weathered face showed her age, but she bounded toward them with the robust energy of a young athlete.

"Good afternoon, Professor." She flung her arms wide and gave him a bear hug. "Gotten yourself into a mess of trouble, haven't you? I figured, sooner or later, you'd come to me."

He hadn't expected such an enthusiastic greeting. He was, after all, a fugitive. Associating with him could cause her trouble. "Are the cops watching your place? Looking for me?"

"As long as you're with me, you're safe."

He wanted to believe her. When he introduced Maxine to Ava, the assistant gave her another all-encompassing hug, followed by the obligatory family connections. "Donovan, eh?"

Surprised, Ava said, "I didn't know you were familiar with Narcissus."

"You betcha. I'm a local, too. Third generation." Maxine combed her fingers through her wild, colorful hair. "You're the baby sister. With those three handsome brothers and your sister, Rachel, who always wins blue ribbons for her pies and cakes. How's your mom? She does crafts, doesn't she?"

"Jewelry," Ava said, looking over Maxine's wares. "She'd love your shop. How did you get into macramé and pottery?"

"It belonged to my great-aunt Marie. When she passed away and left me this building with the shop and apartment included, I decided to move in and keep the family tradition going."

Maxine guided her to a glass case near the cash register and pointed out secondhand jewelry and handmade pieces. Ava's gaze caught on a gold brooch with a Deco pattern of pyramids and roses, which was similar to the design on Georgina's bracelet. "An interesting piece of jewelry. Is it antique?"

"Hmm." Maxine swiveled her head and turned her attention to Liam. "What do you think, Professor?"

THE GOLD BROOCH came from the same salvage operation as the cuff bracelet Quincy had given to his wife. Before they arrived at the shop, Liam had wondered if Maxine would take his side in this tangled situation. Unfortunately, the chunk of stolen jewelry seemed to put her in Stuart's camp. "We both know where that brooch came from."

Her voice took on a falsely innocent tone. "Maybe I've seen this style before."

"Why did you want to meet with me?"

Again with fake naivety, she said, "Why do you think?"

He had neither the time nor the inclination to play guessing games. Maxine had always worked more closely with Stuart than with him. Though Liam thought she hadn't approved of the deceptions Stuart pulled and the lies he required from his assistant, she partnered up with him. Unlikely as it seemed, Ava would have pointed out that Maxine and Stuart were in cahoots.

"I was wrong about you," he said. "I believed you were honest. Sure as hell didn't expect to find out that you were working with Stuart to plunder the salvage we collected. That brooch was stolen from a vessel that sank in the 1920s."

Maxine's artistically drawn eyebrows pulled down in a scowl. "I'm not a thief."

He didn't bother with an argument. "At the very least, you owe me an explanation."

"Fine."

She stuck out her chin. Though not an attractive woman, Maxine had a presence. He wished he could trust her. "Let's hear it."

"I kept that brooch to insure cooperation from Stuart. If the cops came sniffing around, I could flash the jewelry and tell them where it came from. You gotta believe me. I wouldn't think twice about throwing him under the bus."

Liam sensed there was something more she needed to tell him. "And?"

"And I kept something else, too. I have copies of the hand-written ledgers he used—the accurate ledgers as opposed to the fraudulent records of artifacts and objects. I can compare them with the original lists you and the others compiled when you collected salvage."

"You kept an accurate inventory," he said.

"I was a better assistant than you realized."

Those lists and documents proved Stuart's fraud and pointed to other motives for his murder. "How long was this going on?"

"Quite a while," she admitted. "I quit almost a year ago. Also, I have the name and address of the fence in Portland who Quincy was working with."

Liam already knew about Quincy and his Portland contact. "Dammit, Maxine. You should have told me at the time when all this was happening."

"Okay, that was probably a mistake. Sorry."

Anger built inside him. She and Stuart had been cheating him and their clients for years. "Why?"

"Excuse me, Mr. Fancy-Pants, but it didn't seem like a big deal. We didn't take much, and Stuart let me keep some of the pieces, like that brooch. He paid me something on the side to keep quiet about what he was doing. And I liked the bonus." She gestured flamboyantly to her empty shop. "This place isn't exactly a gold mine."

"After I got arrested, why didn't you come forward with this information? The fact that Stuart was engaged in fraud gave a lot of people motive to want him dead."

"Never thought of that." Her eyes widened. This time, her surprised innocence was real. "Oh, God, Liam, now I truly am sorry. I never thought you'd be arrested. Anybody with two brain cells would know that you didn't kill Stuart."

Her vote of confidence came too late. "Who did? Who's the killer?"

Her thick shoulders lifted in a heavy shrug. "I've got no clue."

But she knows something. "I can understand why you didn't want to reveal your part in the scam. Even if it was nothing more than petty theft, you could be charged." He studied her expression, noticing how she avoided looking directly at him. "You're a smart woman, Maxine. Did it occur to you that a rich man like Stuart had no reason to steal trinkets? Why take the risk?"

"I think he got a kick out of doing it. Stuart was an interesting man. He had the soul of a pirate and the detailed penmanship of an eighteenth-century office clerk."

"Do you have the ledgers?"

The jangling bells at the front door announced the arrival of a new customer, and Maxine called out to the woman who entered. "Make yourself at home."

"The ledgers." Liam growled. His patience was at an end.

"Hush, now. I don't want to miss a sale."

He grasped her arm and turned her toward him. With an effort, he kept his voice low. "I'll buy every pot, every knot and every philodendron in this store if you tell me what you're hiding."

"Who says I'm keeping a secret?"

"You don't have to be afraid, Maxine. Stuart is out of the picture. He can't hurt you or get you in trouble."

She scoffed. "Stuart Whitcomb never scared me."

"Then, who?"

"Tancredo."

Chapter Twenty

In the apartment above the store, Liam stood at the window and looked down at the foot traffic on the sidewalk in Nye Beach while he and Ava waited for Maxine to close her shop and join them. Her living space showed as much pizazz as her clothing and hairstyle. Predictably, the decor featured several hanging plants and wall hangings with polished agates and crystals woven in the strands of jute. The patterns for chairs, tablecloths and drapes ranged from wild roses to purple polka dots, to a design that looked like frenzied static.

Ava paced between the kitchenette and the entrance. She'd shed her lavender rain jacket. Somehow, she made a loose-fitting, striped blue shirt and high-rise white jeans look sexy. Or maybe that was just his interpretation.

Bursts of energy exploded from her, and he knew she was watching the clock, counting the minutes and not wanting to be late returning Fish's boat. Or feeding her brother. Her ever-responsible attitude warred with the sultry glances she lobbed in his direction, reassuring him that she was also thinking of the time they'd spend together tonight. Nearly as anxious and eager as he was to take their relationship to the next level, her every movement seemed sensual.

He stepped into her path to block her progress, and she halted midstride. Her forward momentum was such that she bumped into him. When she rested her palms on his chest to steady herself, he took advantage of the moment to embrace her and kiss her forehead. He inhaled deeply. Her curly, brown hair smelled like a garden of fragrant lilac and mint.

"Don't worry," he said. "We'll get back before dark."

"How can anybody think in the midst of this chaos?"

"Are you talking about the details of Stuart's theft or the decor in this room?"

"Both." She fidgeted in his arms. "It's amazing that Maxine was efficient enough to manage the business at Deep Dive."

"She was actually good at her job."

"Even better than you imagined." Ava tilted her head back and sighed. "After she was done with her administrative duties, she had a whole side occupation selling stolen artifacts."

And he was still furious. "When she hands over those ledgers, it's going to open another can of worms. Quincy is involved. He's going to be in serious trouble."

"As long as he stays on Georgina's good side, she'll make sure he has an excellent lawyer."

She squeezed against him. Her breasts flattened against his chest, distracting him from what she was saying. He took a moment to get back on track. "Repeat."

"The important question," she said. "Did Peter Quincy murder Stuart Whitcomb?"

He nodded. "Say more."

"If Stuart threatened to blab about fencing the salvage, Quincy might have wanted to make sure he couldn't tell anybody. Also, Quincy is famous for his hot temper."

Liam gave another nod. Her reasoning fit one of his prior theories that Quincy met Stuart on the boat with the intention of both of them talking to Liam and convincing him to sell his shares in Deep Dive. A phrase popped into his head. "Changed my mind."

"About what?" she asked.

"In one of my visions, I remembered Stuart saying those words. He changed his mind about something."

"Which might have made Quincy angry enough to strike out." Her forehead wrinkled as she considered. "I hate to say it, but Georgina's husband looks pretty good as a suspect."

"I'm not going to be too quick to judge." Maxine had more to tell them about Tancredo. "If Quincy and Stuart wanted to talk to me, why was I drugged?"

When he heard the apartment door open, he gave Ava a peck on the cheek and turned to face Maxine. Her large body wilted under the stress of the situation, but her multicolored hair was energized in an outburst of spikes and curls. When she stomped across the room and flopped onto a colorful love seat, a round orange cat who clashed with the purple polka dots leaped onto her lap and yowled.

"My poor, sweet Melon Ball. You're hungry," Maxine said. "And so am I."

"I wanted to order pizza to take back to the lighthouse," Ava said. "I'd be happy to get you something."

"A meatball sandwich and a calzone," she said. "The phone number for the Italian place on the corner is on the fridge."

While she went to place their order, Liam sat opposite Maxine, leaned forward and stared into her eyes. "I'm not leaving here without those ledgers. I'll try my hardest to keep you out of trouble. My expensive attorney can help. He needs to earn his retainer."

"You always played fair." She grinned. "Not like Stuart who was a terrible horndog, a liar and a cheat. Still, the man had lovely handwriting."

"Tell me about Tancredo."

"People don't pay much attention to the grungy, three-fingered harbormaster who smells like rotten fish. He's always there, always keeping an eye on things. The marina clients with their fancy yachts ignore him unless they have a problem. I'm guessing they consider him beneath them. And the commercial fleets, like Deep Dive, give him his due without realizing that Tancredo is a truly dangerous bastard. For years, he's worked with the drug runners from British Columbia. They're every bit as dangerous and lethal as the cartels in Mexico." She visibly shuddered. "As soon as I found out Tancredo was involved with Quincy and Stuart, I backed off. Quit my job and never looked back."

"How did you find out?"

"I had a message for Stuart. When I contacted him on the dive boat, I learned that Tancredo and Quincy were with him. I don't know for sure if they were picking up drugs for distribution or making an exchange of some sort. Frankly, I didn't want to know."

Liam had heard that Tancredo was on the boat without his knowledge. "Why wasn't I on board? Where was I?"

"Teaching or out of town. Stuart was no dummy. He always made sure you wouldn't catch a whiff of his wrongdoing."

All the sneaking around meant Stuart knew about Tancredo's drug contacts. Liam could almost understand the way Stuart dabbled in criminal activity. Fencing and theft were like a game to him. As Maxine suggested, it seemed harmless. Not as though he'd stolen a pirate chest full of gold doubloons. Drug smuggling was different.

"I've heard," Liam said, "that Tancredo provided drugs to people on the street."

Maxine shifted her bulk and Melon Ball adjusted his position, nudging her hand so she had to stroke his fur. He started purring as loudly as a motorboat. "The harbormaster isn't a drug dealer. He likes his job too much to risk it."

"I was drugged before Stuart's murder," he said. "Probably with something similar to date rape drugs, like Rohypnol. Whatever I was given absorbed quickly into my system and didn't show in a tox screen. It knocked me out. I didn't have any memory at first. Little by little, things are coming back to me."

Maxine shook her head. "I'm so sorry, Liam."

"Could Tancredo have been responsible?"

She and Melon Ball harmonized on a groan. "Yeah, Charlie Tancredo could easily lay hands on those kinds of drugs."

Liam was still having trouble visualizing the unkempt Tancredo as a wily villain. "What about the quarter of a million dollars he loaned to Stuart?"

Taken aback, she narrowed her gaze and stared. "Are you sure about that?"

Liam had found it hard to believe the first time he'd come across the loan in his preliminary research of suspects. But Tancredo himself confirmed the loan when he talked to Ava. And Holly was aware of it. A quarter of a million.

Ava bustled into the front room from the kitchen and grabbed her lavender raincoat. "Okay, I ordered three pizzas, two meatball sandwiches and four calzones."

"That should do it," Maxine said. "For me and my sweet Melon Ball."

"I'll go pick up the order," Ava said.

Liam offered, "Give me a minute, and I'll come with you."

"You stay here and finish your talk. You don't need to rush." She slipped into her coat. "I still haven't been able to contact my brother, but I called Fish and told him not to wait for us. He can take my Sonata from the garage."

He watched her dash out the door. From the time he knew her as a student until now, he'd admired her ability to multitask and organize. He wondered how that talent would play out tonight when they were finally alone.

Maxine loudly cleared her throat in a blatant attempt to get his attention. "Tell me more about this loan from Tancredo."

"The first time I heard about it was when my attorney and private eye collected data on Stuart's finances. The actual cash was difficult to trace, but the valuation was there among his assets."

Her eyebrows lifted. "I'm not altogether sure what you're saying."

"Bookkeeping isn't my strong suit," he admitted. "All I know is that Stuart used a large chunk of the loan to buy his cabin cruiser, *The Reckless.*"

"I've got it!" Maxine slapped her thigh and Melon Ball jumped down. "Tancredo wasn't talking about money. Stuart had something else of his, something worth a huge amount of cash."

"Drugs?"

"Bingo." She bounced to her feet. "Now I understand. Somehow, Stuart had taken control of a valuable stash. Tancredo's merchandise."

"No wonder the harbormaster wanted him dead."

Finally, he had an answer that made sense. Stuart had been involved in double-crossing Tancredo and stealing his drug supplies. A strong motive for murder.

BACK IN FISH'S MOTORBOAT, Ava stashed the pizza feast from Bella Trattoria—minus a meatball sandwich and calzone for Maxine—in a cabinet at the helm. The food would be cold when she delivered it to her brother, but that was why microwaves were invented. As she had predicted, their meeting with Maxine ran long, and she was glad she'd told Fish to take her spare car keys from the rolltop desk and use her Sonata to drive home.

The extra time spent with Maxine Gallo had been well worth it. The flamboyant former assistant had given Liam copies of Stuart's fraudulent inventory ledgers. She'd kept the originals in the wall safe for Knots and Pots. More than the paperwork, she'd clarified the three-way axis with Stuart, Quincy and Tancredo.

While Liam expertly guided the motorboat away from the dock near Nye Beach and headed for the open sea, she reviewed the details. "Let me see if I've got it right," she said. "Stuart partnered up with Quincy, who is also in the salvage business, and the two of them siphoned off pieces of valuable freight they recovered from sunken ships."

"Stuart created a fake inventory. Certain items were never delivered to our warehouse."

"What kind of volume are we talking about?"

"Not much." He shrugged. "Both Deep Dive and Quincy's Salvage are small-time businesses. Neither of us have the heavy-duty equipment necessary for reclaiming large consignments and shipping containers."

As far as she could tell, Stuart had been taking a big risk for a relatively small reward. "Some of your finds were remarkable. Like the gold, Deco-style bracelet and brooch from the ship that went down in the 1920s."

"Not a bad haul," he said. "The jewelry was locked in a safe and belonged to some of the passengers on board. Claims were filed by heirs and estates when we recorded the salvage. The total paid by an insurance adjustor was slightly more than a hundred thousand."

"That's significant."

"And unusual," he said. "Even though maritime archeologists and anthropologists like to think of themselves as sea-faring versions of Indiana Jones, we seldom recover valuable sunken treasure. Maybe only once or twice a year. I wonder if that shipwreck from the 1920s was what tempted Stuart."

"Maybe he just needed money. Holly thought so." Ava couldn't believe Stuart was broke but understood that wealthy families, like Stuart and Serena Whitcomb, often had excessive spending habits. "Your people did the research, is that true?"

"Like a lot of people, Stuart is rich with assets, but he's not liquid. Doesn't have cash in his back pocket. That's why he ran into trouble when he lost Tancredo's drugs."

This part of the story confused her. Did Stuart steal the drugs or lose them? Or was it some kind of loan? "Tell me what happened."

"Maxine and I put our heads together, and this is what we came up with." Cruising due south along the coast, the incoming tide rolled gently and the wind was calm. "Drug distributors from British Columbia used Tancredo as a dispersal point for their shipments. When it wasn't safe for them to come ashore and deal with him directly, they dropped off their cargo in an underwater preselected location, not too hard to locate with the kind of sonar we use at Deep Dive."

"How big are these packages of drugs?" she asked.

"The size could vary from a carry-on bag to a steamer trunk. The contents would have to be carefully packed and sealed to keep out moisture."

"Seems like a simple procedure. They drop it off. Later, Quincy or Stuart go out and make the pickup using their sonar equipment to guide them to the right location."

"Simple." He agreed. "Until something goes wrong."

"And Stuart loses track of a quarter-million-dollar shipment of illegal drugs."

She and Liam batted around theories of what might have happened, ranging from an outright theft by Stuart to an incorrect record of the location, to a sonar or GPS malfunction. Liam concluded, "It might be that I was using the boat for another project and Stuart couldn't get it alone."

"I don't think we'll find out unless Quincy or Tancredo tells us."

"That's not going to happen."

She leaned back in her seat and tilted her head toward the late afternoon sun in the west. The saltwater breeze cooled her skin. The low-pitched rumble of the motor created a subtle background of sound. Zipping across the waves, she enjoyed a feeling of weightlessness as though floating.

As their investigation drew to a close, her tension eased. She exhaled a long sigh and relaxed. Surely, they'd uncovered enough evidence to clear Liam of the murder charges. Though they didn't know who had come aboard *The Reckless* and bludgeoned Stuart, it had to be either Quincy or Tancredo—men with criminal intent and lots of motive.

When their little motorboat neared Cape Absolute, her gaze fixed on the lighthouse. In spite of the scrawls of graffiti, the tower stood tall and proud at the edge of the cliff. The ever-present seabirds soared from their rock and swooped above the waves. They were almost close enough to hear the barking of the sea lions. She felt like they were coming home to a special place for her and Liam.

"I'm glad this is almost over." She scooted closer to him and glided her hand down his muscular arm. "Everything turned out well."

"And it's about to get better."

He enfolded her in his arms, lowered his head and nuzzled her cheek. His stubble was scratchy, and she giggled before she flung her arms around his neck and kissed him hard. Though preoccupied with guiding the boat safely to shore, he returned her kiss. The ocean winds swirled around them, but he was hot, flaming hot. She pressed the length of her body against him, needing a full connection. Her leg straddled his thigh.

"Ava, my bright star," he whispered in a husky voice. "I've wanted this for so very long."

"Yes," she responded, unable to come up with anything more intelligent. Now wasn't the time to be smart. Now was about pure sensation. "Yes, yes."

In a wide swoop, he circled the massive offshore rock and cut the speed so he could maneuver in the narrow space between the rock and the shore. The sound of the motor faded to a gentle putt-putt-putt. He glided the boat to a perfect stop beside the short dock.

Before they ran aground or crashed into the wood pilings, he leaped out and tied the line to the cleat. Just as quickly, he was back in the boat beside her. He gave long, lingering attention to their kiss. Tearing open her lavender rain jacket, he hauled her closer to kiss and fondle. With every touch, her body came more alive. She trembled when he nibbled at her earlobe.

More than anything, she wanted to be alone with him, to give him everything he wanted and to take his attentions in return. With huge reluctance she pulled away. Her unfocused gaze centered on his rugged features. Breathing hard, she stammered, "I—I—I gotta f-f-feed Michael. He's probably starved."

"Your brother can wait."

But she couldn't. "Open that cabinet. Give me two of the pizzas. And a calzone."

"Wait for another minute and I'll come with you."

"Bring the rest of the food." If she didn't go now, she never would. And she couldn't disappoint Michael. She'd been making dinner for her brothers since she was a kid. "Let me dash up to the cottage. I'll meet you back at the lighthouse."

She slipped the backpack with her phone over her shoulder, grabbed the food and jogged across the sand to the path leading up to the cottage. At the brink of sunset, many of the sea lions had already abandoned their rock to forage for dinner and find a warmer place to sleep. Likewise, the nesting birds were settling in for the evening.

She and Liam weren't much different from the other animals. Creatures of habit. Tonight, they'd create their own special ritual for making love. Slowly, they'd discover the secrets of their bodies. Then, in a rising crescendo, they would fulfill their mutual longing and desire.

It would be epic.

Charging up the hill, she was breathing hard as she approached the lightkeeper's cottage. In the side parking area, she saw Michael's yellow Jeep Wrangler and another vehicle. The classy, gray Escalade had vanity plates that read: MSTR Q.

Under her breath, she whispered an out-of-character curse. "Damn you, Peter Quincy."

Chapter Twenty-One

Ava couldn't believe Quincy had come here. On their way to Nye Beach, she'd left a message on his phone telling him that their scheduled meeting for tomorrow was canceled. He had no valid reason for showing his face at the lighthouse. Damn, damn, double damn, hell.

Put a lid on it. Growing up and dealing with the frequent frustration of three brothers and a sister, Ava had made a rule for herself. No swearing. Otherwise, every other word out of her mouth would be profane.

Quincy was here. And she needed to deal with him. She glanced toward the path from the beach. Liam hadn't yet appeared. Should she run back and tell him? But she'd be wasting precious time. Michael was in the house with the man who might have murdered Stuart.

Setting down the pizza boxes, she took the phone from her backpack. Her fingers hovered over the screen. Marshal Woodburn's phone number was in her contacts. She might need him for backup, but when Woodburn showed up, he'd have to take Liam into custody. A phone call to law enforcement would signal the end of the greatly anticipated, well-deserved evening in her beloved fugitive's arms.

Her first move: check out the situation and get accurate details. It was possible that Quincy and Michael were sitting and talking while they shared a beer. Circling the house, she crept up to the windows in the parlor with the big-screen television. She heard the broadcast of the Seattle Mariners baseball game. This early in the season, hopes ran high for a brilliant year. Michael had already lectured her about how the signature team for the Pacific Northwest would come through and win the World Series.

Hoping everything was normal, she searched through the construction clutter, spotted an empty ten-gallon bucket, which she hauled to the windows and flipped over. She climbed on top and peeked inside. Her brother and Fish Finley were lying on the worn carpet with hands tied behind their backs and ankles bound with gray duct tape. For a moment, her heart stopped. Were they okay? If Michael had been injured, she'd never forgive herself. She'd dragged him into this mess.

Then she saw Fish wiggle his shoulders. Michael's eyes were closed, but he was also moving. She didn't see blood. Didn't notice any kind of injury.

A gravelly voice rumbled behind her. "Step down from that bucket. No funny business."

"What have you done to them?"

She looked over her shoulder and saw Tancredo with a pistol clenched in his good hand. His presence scared her far more than an appearance by Quincy. Georgina's husband was a creep and a gold digger, but he cultivated a gentlemanly attitude as befitted the lord of the Solomon manor. Clean and well-dressed, he didn't strike immediate fear into her heart.

On the other hand, Tancredo with his stringy gray hair and grizzled jowls, looked like he'd crawled out of the sewer. Though he stood several yards away, she could smell the stench of rotted fish.

He growled and spat. "Your boys are going to be fine.

When they wake up, they won't remember what hit them. Didn't feel a damn thing."

Exactly what had happened to Liam. "You drugged them."

"You're welcome." He wheezed a chuckle. "If I hadn't knocked them out, they'd be witnesses, and I'm not stupid. I can't leave anybody behind to send me to jail."

It didn't bode well for her that he wasn't making an effort to hide his identity. Ava feared she was expendable. Looking down at the phone in her hand, she pressed the call signal for Marshal Woodburn. "What do you want from me?"

"Get down off that bucket and turn around so I can see your pretty face."

She did as he said, angling her arm behind her back so he wouldn't see her phone. She doubted Woodburn would answer but hoped his voice mail would record her message and alert him to where she was and what kind of danger she was in. Instead, someone else picked up and told her she'd reached the US Marshal Service.

Speaking loudly so her phone would pick up her voice, Ava said, "You don't scare me, Charlie Tancredo."

"Then you're a fool, Ava."

"How dare you come here to the lighthouse and threaten me. You must know there are people keeping a watch on this place, people like Marshal Woodburn." She desperately hoped her loud message was getting through. "They're looking for Dr. Liam Brody."

"What kind of game are you playing?" He took a step toward her. "You got something in your hand. Show me."

"Get away from me, Tancredo." She stepped back, putting more distance between them. "Don't point that gun at me."

"Show me your hands."

He grabbed her arm with his three-fingered hand and shook her. The phone fell to the ground. With his waterproofed, steel-toed workman's boot, he stomped the screen. Swerving his lanky body with surprising agility, he flung her to the damp ground and aimed the barrel of his handgun at her head.

Instinct told her to close her eyes. To curl into a ball and bury her head in her arms like a child afraid of the boogeyman. But she refused to die like a coward. Ava didn't look away. Her jaw set, and her eyes focused. If she was about to die, she wanted to see the bullet coming.

He squeezed the trigger. The shot exploded.

Though she felt no pain, Ava froze. Her ears rang with the reverberation of the gunshot.

She stared at Tancredo. His baggy pants hung low on his scrawny hipbones. His filthy jacket that had once been beige was unbuttoned. Underneath, he wore a black wet suit.

"Come out, Professor," he yelled. "I want to see you now. Or the next shot goes right between her big, blue eyes."

When Liam walked around the corner of the house with hands raised, her pulse fluttered and her breath caught in her throat. She wanted to believe he'd rescue her, but it was more likely that he just signed his death warrant.

In a totally calm voice, he asked, "Where's Quincy? I see his car but don't see him."

"I don't need him. That joker has been out to hornswoggle me from the get-go."

"Did you steal his car?"

"Don't need his damn luxury vehicle. I came here in my inflatable. That boat gets me around just fine." He waved his gun in Liam's direction. "You, of all people, should know that."

"You killed Stuart."

"Shut the hell up," Tancredo yelled.

She watched Liam's face change expression. He went from

rage to comprehension and back to anger. "It was you on *The Reckless*. Finally, I recognize your voice."

Ava scrambled to her feet and ran to him. She pressed herself against him so tightly that she could feel the interplay of muscles in his chest and breathe in his masculine scent. Everything about him was so right. Together, they were near perfection.

Tancredo made his wheezing cackle. "I knew you'd remember. It was only a matter of time. The amnesia from those drugs doesn't last forever, and I saw you watching while Stuart and I were going at each other."

"You shouted," Liam said. "I heard your words grate in the back of your throat before you bludgeoned him. I witnessed the murder."

"Real clever, Professor. Give yourself a gold star." His lip curled in a sneer. "Stuart Whitcomb got what he deserved. Payback was long overdue."

Ava remembered Tancredo's grudge against the Whitcomb family. He blamed the grandfather for cheating Stuart's ancestor out of what should have been his rightful inheritance. The harbormaster must have been nursing that hostility his whole life. He even blamed Stuart for the loss of his fingers. "Is this about what happened to your grandfather?"

"That and more. This was about the loan."

"The drugs," Liam said. "Call it what it was. Not an aboveboard loan but lethal narcotics. Somehow Stuart swindled you out of a significant amount of illegal drugs."

"I'm not sure if he meant to cheat me or if he just wasn't good at handling the sonar equipment." Tancredo gestured with the gun. "Go that way, down to the shore. We're going to take a little cruise."

Ava didn't like where this story was leading. "What do you want from us?"

"Your boyfriend is going to have a chance to play the hero," he said. "We're going on a treasure hunt. We'll go to the harbor, pick up his dive boat and head out to sea."

"To retrieve your lost shipment of drugs," Liam said.

"Figured it out, did you? You're a hell of a lot smarter than Whitcomb. I should have hooked up with you instead of your partner. You're going to get into your boat, read the GPS data and take me where I want to go."

Ava couldn't believe this. Was that supposed to be a compliment? As if Liam would agree to help Tancredo and drug runners from the north. His sick appreciation disgusted her. When he waved his gun again, Liam refused to move. She felt his muscles tense and prayed he wouldn't do anything that caused Tancredo to attack.

Gently, he moved her away from him and turned to face Tancredo. "Why the hell do you think I'd help you?"

"If you don't, Ava will pay the price. She'll die slowly. My first shot will tear off two fingers on her left hand. She'll share my pain."

More than the pain, she feared Tancredo's cruelty. He'd kill them both. In her mind, their only chance came from staying alive as long as possible, hoping that Woodburn got the message and came racing to their rescue. "Let's go, Liam."

Tancredo wheezed a laugh. "You heard the lady. She goes first down the path, then you follow. Me and my .44 Magnum will bring up the rear."

Forcing herself not to falter, she struck out toward the path leading down to the beach. The steep, rocky incline wasn't easy to descend in the semidarkness as dusk fell, and she moved cautiously. Somehow, she needed to talk to Liam and tell him not to resist. She'd summoned backup and had to believe Marshal Woodburn would be here.

But Liam had ideas of his own. He moved up quickly behind her and caused her to stumble. As he helped her up, he whispered, "When I give the signal, run like hell for the far end of the beach. I'll deal with Tancredo."

"You can't take him. He's got a gun."

"Run as fast as you can. Don't look back."

Desperately, she said, "I won't leave you."

Gunfire blasted behind them, and Tancredo yelled, "Break it up, you two."

He shoved away from her. "You can do this. I love you."

No, no, no, no. This wasn't supposed to happen this way. They were supposed to spend a splendid night together and declare their intentions.

She staggered forward. When she reached the bottom of the path and her feet hit sand, the few sea lions on the rock set up a racket, distracting Tancredo. The gulls circled and cried out as they watched the drama.

Liam called to her, "Go, Ava. Now."

Without thinking, she burst into a sprint. Her back prickled, and she feared she'd be shot at any moment. She heard Liam struggling with Tancredo. Faster, she needed to go faster. She dodged to the edge of the surf where the sand was firmly packed.

In the distance, she saw the inflatable boat Tancredo had hauled ashore. His timing was bad. The incoming tide lapped at the edge of his craft.

She heard a loud moan, someone crying for help. And she turned toward the rocky shore. A long, weathered drift-wood log rested near the hillside. A person sprawled against it. His blood-covered hand reached toward her and then fell to his side.

She recognized Quincy. A harpoon from a spear gun stuck out from his upper chest. Tancredo must have shot him and left him there to bleed out. Her horror faded to silence when she spotted the handgun on the sand beside him.

Quincy's head slumped forward onto his chest. Barely conscious, he was too weak to move, but his gun might be their salvation. She dashed toward him and scooped up the weapon, which was much bigger and harder to handle than her neon pink Glock.

Unsure of how to handle the weapon and wishing she'd taken lessons on marksmanship, she spun around. Down the beach, she saw Liam and Tancredo locked in a hand-to-hand struggle. The heavy weapon hung loosely in her hand. She couldn't fire at Tancredo without endangering Liam.

Instead, she aimed at the sky and let go with four shots. The noise echoed across the Pacific like thunder. Both combatants turned toward her.

Liam took advantage of the distraction to deliver a ferocious blow to the old man's jaw. Tancredo's legs crumpled, and he went down. Liam ripped the gun from his good hand.

She raced toward them, watching as Liam lowered the barrel of the gun to aim at the scrawny chest of the grizzled, old harbormaster. She flung herself into his arms.

Not taking his eyes off Tancredo, he kissed the top of her head. "We won."

"I love you, too."

But they wouldn't spend tonight together. Marshal Woodburn led a posse of law enforcement officers onto the path and down to the beach. He took charge of arresting Tancredo and summoning ambulances and EMTs to help Quincy as well as her brother and Fish. After he disarmed Liam and took her gun, he regretfully cuffed Liam.

"Sorry, Professor."

"I never meant to be this much trouble."

"Sure you did." Woodburn grinned and smoothed his

thick, gray mustache. "Was it worth it? Did you find what you were looking for?"

He gazed into Ava's eyes. "Everything I wanted and more."

Three weeks later...

THE MURDER CHARGES against Liam were dropped, but he was still under house arrest for violating his parole. He'd pleaded guilty and fully expected to be sentenced with a heavy fine and community service for his days as a fugitive. No price was too high. The time he'd spent with Ava changed his life for the better.

Marshal Woodburn didn't bother with handcuffs when he drove Liam from the jail to his mid-century modern home in the hills outside Eugene. "You can't ever tell anyone I admitted this," he said, "but I'm proud of your investigation. Your evidence put Tancredo out of business, and the harbormaster rolled over for the DEA and exposed a ring of narcotics dealers and smugglers."

Liam nodded. "My goal was justice for Stuart, but I'm glad for the more far-reaching benefits."

Quincy's injury put him in the hospital for two solid weeks, but he didn't seem to have permanent damage. And Georgina had taken him back. Charges against him were still pending, and he'd probably never use that fence in Portland again. With help from Liam's pricy attorney, Maxine's involvement in fencing had been pretty much erased in exchange for her ledgers filled with proof of wrongdoing.

Fish Finley had been running Deep Dive for the past three weeks, ably assisted by Oliver Whitcomb. Both were turning out to be great assets, capable of keeping things operating when Liam got back to work at the university or went far afield to do research.

He stretched his shoulders and gazed through the windshield at the spring landscape. Fresh green leaves of trees and shrubs were highlighted by blooming rhododendrons in vivid purple, yellow, white and orange. Fluffy clouds hung low over the peaks of the wooded Cascades. The incredible, natural beauty of the land surrounding his home excited him, but the joy surging through him came from a different source. Finally, he would see Ava. He'd hold her in his arms. Tonight, they would finally—finally!—make love.

She'd been quick to forgive him, though she'd been charged with aiding and abetting a fugitive and pleaded guilty. Her sentence—expected to be a hefty fine and parole—would be decided later. She'd visited him twice in jail before they decided it was too frustrating to see each other and not be able to touch. He had planned for this reunion, including the purchase of a perfect diamond engagement ring that Woodburn had kept safe for him. For hours every day, Liam practiced how he would propose to her.

Paused at a stoplight, Woodburn said, "I want you to know, Liam, that you really aren't a criminal mastermind and local law enforcement isn't completely inept. With the possible exception of Jess-hole."

"You knew about his nickname?"

"I know about everything."

Liam immediately understood. "You were watching while we solved the crime. You gave me a chance to prove my innocence."

"And if you tell anybody, I'll deny it." He reached into his jacket pocket and produced a small velvet box. "I expect you're going to need this before you see Ava."

"Is she waiting at the house?"

"Couldn't keep her away. She said something about serving you a dinner that was cooked by her sister, Rachel, the blue-ribbon baker."

"Great." Food wasn't the first thing on his mind.

"I'll stop by tomorrow to hook up your ankle bracelet. Don't leave the property."

With Ava here, he had no other place he wanted to be. As they cruised through the forest surrounding his house, he saw her on the front porch. She waved with both arms and charged at the car as soon as Woodburn parked.

He caught her on the fly and held her. Overwhelmed, he absorbed the moment. Finally, they were together, the way they had always been meant to be.

Though he'd intended to wait until after dinner when the sun was setting behind the mountains and a soft breeze tickled the leaves, Liam didn't make it any farther than the front porch. He dropped to one knee. On the flat of his hand, he held the velvet box. Gently, he opened the lid and took out the ring.

She pulled back her hand. "Wait."

"Something wrong?" His throat was dry. "What is it, Ava?"

"We have to wait until after Christmas."

"Why?"

"The renovations will be done by then. I want to get married in the lighthouse."

"I wouldn't have it any other way."

He slipped the ring on her finger.

* * * * *